SEAL
WITH A KISS

SEAL
WITH A KISS

•

Jessica Andersen

AVALON BOOKS
NEW YORK

© Copyright 2003 by Jessica Andersen
Library of Congress Catalog Card Number: 2003093922
ISBN 0-8034-9623-0
Published by Thomas Bouregy & Co., Inc.
160 Madison Avenue, New York, NY 10016

PRINTED IN THE UNITED STATES OF AMERICA
ON ACID-FREE PAPER
BY HADDON CRAFTSMEN, BLOOMSBURG, PENNSYLVANIA

To my dad, Todd Andersen, for his support.

Chapter One

"Thar she blows!"

Smitty glanced up at the crow's nest of the research vessel *Streaker* and grinned. Ishmael might not be a cheeky intern any more, but the kid still couldn't resist showing off when he pulled spyglass duty. Knowing what was coming next, Smitty yelled, "What do you see, Ishmael?"

"*Globicephala melaena*, sir!"

Smitty quickly ran through his spotty memory of Miss Peach's Latin class. Shoot. It wasn't one of the marine mammals commonly spotted off Cape Cod by *Streaker* and the members of Dolphin Friendly. The Latin was unfamiliar, and he was darned if he was going to let the kid win this time. Ishmael was already ahead five to three on this voyage, having stumped him on white-sided dolphins and a herring gull.

He still thought the herring gull was cheating.

But this one . . . he could just see three puffs of white at the horizon, a sure sign of marine mammals. Aware that the clock was ticking, he ran the words through his mind again. *Globicephala malaena. Cephala* was easy—that was "head," and he figured anything with "globe" in it had to be round. Okay. Round-headed *melaena.* "What the heck kind of Latin is *melaena*?" he muttered to himself.

Unfortunately, the words were heard by the bane of his existence. The hair shirt of his world. The pea under his mattress. The little rock inside the shoe of his life.

Violet Oliver.

"It's not Latin, darling. It's Greek for 'black,' as in black, round-headed *long-finned pilot whales.*" She flicked her shiny brunette hair in the way that hadn't failed to annoy him once in the many years they'd worked together. "And that puts you down six to three, unless I'm mistaken."

And Smitty knew that Violet never made mistakes.

He seethed a little as he watched her glide across the deck in a shortie wetsuit that only one tenth of one percent of the population of the world could possibly look good wearing.

Violet, of course, looked incredible. Then again, Violet always looked great.

Even at the end of a weeklong run, when Smitty's hair was standing on end, his clothes were stuck to him with a combination of salt water and general grunge, and his teeth felt like they had acquired a layer of shag carpeting, Violet would look perfect. Her hair would be clean and slightly curled, her fingernails and toenails cheerfully painted, and her clothes freshly pressed.

He was pretty sure she did it just to irritate him.

There had been another time, in what now seemed like another life, when they had been close. Violet, Brody Davenport, and Smitty had been thrown together in the marine mammal program of U.C. Santa Cruz and had become a trio of friends that had seemed inseparable until—

"Hey Smitty, wake up."

Fingers snapped in front of his nose and Smitty blinked, focusing on *Streaker's* pristine deck, on the endless ocean surrounding them, and on the face of the last of that trio, Brody Davenport. "Yeah, boss?"

Though Smitty and Violet were Ph.D.'s with mile-long resumes of their own, Brody was the idea man, the politician, and the acknowledged leader of Dol-

phin Friendly. Smitty was content to be the man behind the scenes. He was the organizer, the planner,
the guy who got things done and kept the boat lively.

Brody began, "I want—"

Streaker pulled to within a few hundred feet of the
long-finned pilot whales and Brody forgot what he
was going to say.

Smitty grinned. He knew the feeling. The all-
consuming awe they felt in the presence of marine
mammals was the glue that kept their little group
together through thick and thin, ups and downs.

And there had been plenty of each over the years.

The pod contained maybe thirty animals, ranging
from five or six feet in length to over twenty feet,
and as the members of Dolphin Friendly watched, a
pair of round black heads broke the surface and the
lighter gray of the animals' throats glowed against
the blue-green North Atlantic water.

While not uncommon in the waters off Smugglers
Cove, the long-finned pilot whales never failed to
enthrall Smitty.

"Quick, Violet, get the camera! I have a feeling
something good's going to happen," Brody hissed.
"And get Maddy from the sonar room, she won't
want to miss this."

Brody's wife had joined the team recently and
Smitty thought it rather sweet the way his boss

wanted to share everything with her. Sweet and vaguely unsettling. Where once *Streaker* had belonged to the three original members of Dolphin Friendly, with a rotating cast of interns coming and going, the dynamic had changed after Brody's marriage.

Now it was a pair of pairs.

Understandably, Brody wanted to spend time with his wife, but that left Smitty alone with . . . Violet. He glanced over as she returned with the waterproof video camera and he found himself nose to lens with the thing.

"Smile for the camera, Smitty," she trilled, knowing full well he hated to have his picture taken. He scowled as the little red light blinked to indicate that it was recording the sight of him: sunburned nose, diving mask marks, bad hair decade, and all.

Either his skin had grown thinner, or her digs had become more frequent of late, because he felt his patience fading fast. His voice rose as he said, "Violet, why don't you take that camera and—"

"There you are!" Maddy put a hand on his arm and pulled him away. "I was hoping you could explain what we're seeing right now. Do pilot whales often congregate in groups of this size?"

Smitty looked down into Maddy's guileless eyes and snorted as she towed him to the other end of the boat. "Bull-oney. You just finished your degree, so you're bound to know as much about this as I do, if not more. But I'm grateful for the interruption." He sighed and glanced back at Violet, who was chatting with Brody as she panned the camera across the lively ocean. "We're getting on each other's nerves more and more these days. I think once the Smugglers Cove Stranding Center is up and running and we expand the Dolphin Friendly fleet, Violet and I should take different boats for a while. If we spend much more time together, I'm afraid we'll kill each other or something."

Though it pained him to say the words, the truth was inescapable. He and Violet were like oil and water. While the combination used to mix just fine, it had stopped working about the time Brody and Maddy got married.

Smitty didn't like to think of what that might mean, just as he didn't like to remember that Violet and Brody had once dated.

Maddy smiled and patted his arm. "Personally, I think I'd bet on the 'or something' happening between you and Violet, and it might be the best thing for both of you."

With a final grin, Maddy walked over to where Brody was hanging over the rail with a boom mike to pick up the squalls of the pilot whales. Watching her go, Smitty muttered, "What the heck does that mean?"

He glanced at Violet with her turquoise neoprene, her waterproof camera, and her talent for irritating him from twenty feet away, and shook his head.

Or something.

Smitty was looking at her again. Violet could feel it like an itch. A rash. Like poison ivy or a jellyfish sting, he got under her skin and lurked there, waiting for her to let her guard down and let him in. In defiance, she aimed the camera directly at him, knowing that he would duck and run, though what he had against cameras was beyond her. He looked great in pictures.

Whenever he was caught in a candid photograph, Smitty always looked like one of those rugged male models posing for companies that sold camping gear and expensive polo shirts. His windblown auburn hair was bleached white at the tips, and his eternally tanned face was free of freckles and creased with interesting lines.

She hated those lines. They reminded her of how long she'd known him. How long it had been since he'd chosen Ellen over her. How long she'd been trying to forget him and move on with her life.

She spun her camera in Smitty's direction a second time, hoping to annoy him again.

But he didn't run. He wasn't paying attention to her after all, darn him. He stared out to sea, at the half-dozen bottle-nosed dolphins that had joined the pilot whales and were gamboling around the larger animals, playing in *Streaker's* shadow.

"Hey Violet, get some film of these guys. We still need five or six minutes of tape to run behind Brody's voice-over at the beginning of the opening ceremony video." Smitty waved at a pair of younger dolphins playing tag, leaping around and over one of the pilot whales. "This would be perfect."

"Don't tell me what to do," she replied with a toss of her hair, "I'm the photographer here, not you."

Then, of course, she had to film the juveniles because he was right, dang it. The dolphins' playful antics were a perfect backdrop to their fearless leader's speech about marine mammal conservation and the purpose of the Smugglers Cove Stranding Center, which was to open in five days amidst much hoopla.

Out of the corner of her eye, Violet saw Brody frown at her. She knew that the constant bickering between his two senior crew members bothered the leader of Dolphin Friendly, and out of fondness for her boss and former—very briefly—boyfriend, Violet might have laid off. She'd even tried to be nice to Smitty a few times recently, but it had been a wasted effort. He'd gone out of his way to annoy her and they'd fallen right back into the same old pattern.

But ever since he had married Maddy, Brody had been on a mission to make Smitty and Violet get along whether they liked it or not. Violet was pretty sure it had been Maddy's idea, since Brody's wife was one of those flowers-and-sunshine kind of people who wanted everyone to be happy.

Well, Violet was plenty happy. Particularly when she was scrapping with her arch-nemesis.

She still owed him for crazy-gluing her swim fins to the deck last week. And she didn't think he'd used his snorkel since she dipped the mouthpiece in that hotter-than-blazes jalapeño sauce.

Smiling at the thought, she continued to film the dolphins playing around the pilot whales. In frame, Smitty leaned over the railing to wave at the animals, and as the sun began to drop low, a magnificent pastel wash of color spread across the sky. The younger dolphins leaped and spun in glorious abandon and Smitty faced the camera, his silhouette expressing the sheer joy of the moment.

"Is there anything better in the world than this?" he yelled. He spread his hands wide, threw his head back, and laughed in wonder, and the two dolphins burst from the water in tandem and corkscrewed in the air just behind him.

From Violet's vantage point, it looked as if the bottlenoses had leaped from the water at his summons, like he was the sorcerer's apprentice. The moment seemed to freeze in time for a heartbeat. Another. Then Smitty dropped his hands and the dolphins fell back to the sea. A single gull flew across the sky and was gone, a black silhouette against the pastel sky.

Then life returned to normal. The pilot whales breathed at the surface once, twice, then rolled and dove into the ocean. The sun set in earnest and the sky lost its magical light. And Smitty became, once again, just a man.

"Did you get that?"

Violet started at the voice, not knowing that Brody had come up behind her while she was engrossed in her filming.

She nodded, not quite ready to trust her voice. The beauty of that moment was still etched on her retinas, the memory still too fresh to be spoken.

"Good. That will be the first scene of the opening ceremony video. If that doesn't convince those politicians to approve our grant, I don't know what will." Brody patted her arm. "Take good care of that film, Violet. It's irreplaceable. I think it might just be the ticket to the second half of our funding."

She nodded again, still not trusting her voice.

"What's the matter, catfish got your tongue?"

Violet started, more violently this time. Smitty had snuck up on her while she was talking to Brody. His presence jangled along her nerve endings and that itch returned, making her irritable and a little bit sad.

When would she be able to be in Smitty's presence and not feel the regret? Probably never.

"Huh?" *Brilliant,* she thought. *Witty repartee at its best.* She drew a breath for another volley, but he beat her to it.

"I'm irreplaceable." He jerked a thumb at his chest and grinned. "Didn't you hear? So if you had any thoughts of replacing me. . . ."

She curled her lip and dangled the camera by one finger. "Well, there had been some talk of this trained monkey at Seaquarium Florida. They say he can whistle 'Ode to Joy' while riding a tricycle. I thought he'd make a nice addition to the team."

Smitty shrugged, and his red hair seemed to glow in the fading light. "Whatever makes you happy, babe."

"Children, play nice." Brody's voice was a mild warning.

Violet felt her fingers tighten on the camera strap. Temper tangled with the last vestiges of the awe she'd felt while filming that scene. "You have no idea what makes me happy, Smitty. You never did."

To her surprise, he didn't rise to the bait and remind her that at one time he'd known exactly how
to make her happy. Instead he turned and walked
away, calling over his shoulder, "Be careful with that
film, Violet darling. I wouldn't want you to wake up
one morning with it crazy-glued to your forehead."

He was so smug. So aggravating. So not interested
in her. With a snarl she spun, intending to stomp
back to the sonar room and slam the door for good
effect.

But she had forgotten about the camera. Dangling
from its strap, the expensive piece of equipment
swung out when she turned. It hit the wheelhouse
wall with a sharp *crack*!

"No!" Violet dove for the deck. Smitty looked
back at her cry.

"Grab it!" He leaped for the camera and barely
managed to graze it with his fingertips as it bounced
once, twice on the deck, ricocheted off a docking
cleat—

And fell overboard.

Smitty lunged for it, and Violet grabbed the back
of his shirt and saved him from following the camera
into the ocean. She would have cursed, would have
apologized, would have given anything to rewind
time a few seconds, but she could do none of those
things. She could only climb to her feet and stand,

awkwardly looking at the deck between her feet while the silence grew thick.

She'd really done it this time.

Brody had needed that film, and if she wasn't mistaken, the camera's waterproof casing had cracked on the first bounce. The new vidcam had become an expensive dolphin toy, the video was toast, and it was all her fault.

She drew a breath. "Brody, I'm—"

"It was my fault."

Violet wasn't the only one on the boat whose jaw dropped when Smitty stepped up beside her and faced Brody's I've-had-just-about-enough-of-you-two look.

Smitty continued, "It wouldn't have happened if I hadn't been needling her, but don't worry. I'll go get the camera. With any luck, the tape'll be salvageable." He disappeared down the stairs and returned a moment later with his diving duffel. The others stood around, looking anywhere but at Brody, whose scowl threatened to melt the deck.

Smitty pulled his swim fins out of the old canvas bag and stuck them on his feet without bothering to change out of his cutoffs and T-shirt. Grinning at Violet, he whispered, "You owe me one, babe."

She could do nothing but nod. Had the world come to an end? Had hell frozen over, pigs flown, and right whale populations suddenly blossomed?

Smitty was saving her bacon.

He jumped into the darkening water with a jaunty wave. His entrance was greeted by chattering clicks from the dolphins that had been bumping the floating yellow, formerly waterproof camera around like a volleyball. Pulling his goggles over his eyes, Smitty adjusted the angle of the snorkel as it curved around behind his head.

Waving, he yelled, "No prob. Just let me rescue my irreplaceable image from Dolphin Friendly's friendly dolphins!"

As he twisted the flexible breathing tube and put the snorkel into his mouth, Violet suddenly remembered.

The hot sauce.

"Smitty, no!" she yelled, but it was too late.

The figure in the water jerked and started thrashing around, emitting horrible gargling sounds and clutching at his mask and snorkel. The water foamed white and the dolphins darted away.

Maddy yelled, "Shark!" and the boat was suddenly abuzz with running figures and yelling people.

"No! No, it's not a shark." Violet waved her arms until some semblance of calm was restored. She could forgive Brody's wife for her paranoia—her parents had been killed by a great white—but the added chaos wasn't helping. She waved her arms again until she had everyone's attention. "Not a shark! He's fine."

"Doesn't look fine," observed Ishmael, pointing at Smitty, who had shed his mask and snorkel and was now gargling with seawater and glaring at Violet through red-rimmed eyes.

"He'll *be* fine," she corrected, and winced at the ire building in Brody's face. "It's only a little jalapeño sauce. He's just being a baby about it."

That earned her an irate splutter from the water and she winced again when she heard Smitty climbing up the rope ladder on *Streaker's* port side. She was in for it.

"He glued my fins to the floor last week. I was just getting him back." Even to Violet that sounded weak. "I . . . I didn't mean for anything bad to happen."

She never did. Somehow, it happened anyway.

Brody rolled his eyes to the heavens as if praying for patience. He stabbed a finger at the crow's nest. "Ishmael, get down here and fetch that camera. It's probably trash, but we don't want to litter. And you two." He divided his glare between Smitty and Violet. "I'll see you in my office in five minutes."

Smitty glanced at Violet and mouthed, "Uh-oh," and she had the insane urge to giggle, though her heart thumped at his teasing. It was like being sent to the principal's office at the age of thirty-two, and that was just plain ridiculous.

Because honestly, what was the worst Brody could do to them?

Chapter Two

Smitty tried not to squirm as his oldest and best friend glared at him from across the chart table in the wheelhouse. If he could go back and undo the last twenty minutes, he would. But it wasn't an option. So he hung his head in real dismay and waited for the explosion.

Brody shook his head in disgust, calmer than Smitty had expected him to be. Maddy must have soothed him a bit. She had a knack for that.

"I don't know what's gotten into you two," Brody began. "You've been at each other night and day for months now and it has to stop. You're affecting morale on the boat and it's impacting your abilities to do your jobs."

While he might argue the morale point, since Ishmael and Maddy were the only other scientists on *Streaker* and they didn't seem to care about the continued tension, Smitty couldn't very well defend his own actions. He'd known he was pushing Violet too hard, but something about the way she'd jumped when he'd walked up behind her had just plain rubbed him wrong and he'd reacted.

Nothing had changed in the decade or so since she'd walked away from what they'd had together. But since Brody's marriage, he'd been thinking more and more about the way he and Violet had ended things. He'd been wishing things were different, and maybe he'd been picking on her because they weren't different. Because he was frustrated. And because the happy couple's relationship showed him what he didn't have.

But now, five spectacular minutes of badly needed footage had paid the price. The camera dripped on the chart table, a long crack in the waterproof casing giving mute testimony to its demise.

"We'll pay for the camera and we'll get another good scene for your video," he offered lamely, aware of Violet standing stiffly nearby.

Brody sighed heavily and ran a hand through his

hair, leaving it sticking up and on end. "How? The opening ceremony is less than a week away. The politicians will be coming to see how we've used the first half of the funding and decide whether to give us the rest. Need I remind you how badly we need that money for the second boat and additional manpower? The Smugglers Cove Stranding Research Center isn't going to get all the way off the ground without it."

"I'm sorry, Brody." They were the first words Violet had spoken since she'd yelled for him not to use his snorkel.

Smitty had to admit that the hot sauce, while surprising and not at all pleasant, had been an excellent practical joke. It was almost as good as the time he had safety pinned her into her hammock and sounded the fire alarm.

Over the years, the practical jokes they'd played on each other had been one of the few links they'd been able to maintain.

Unfortunately, the timing of this particular joke had been just plain bad, and the opening ceremony video had paid the price. But, thought Smitty, everything was fixable.

He sent Violet an encouraging smile, but she didn't notice. Her attention was focused on Brody.

Always Brody. Smitty sighed. Some things, it

seemed, weren't fixable, no matter how hard he wished for it.

"What am I going to do with you two?" Brody asked.

Although he figured it was probably a rhetorical question, Smitty answered, "Keelhaul us? No, seriously, boss. We're very sorry about the videotape and we'll do whatever it takes to make it up to you."

Violet nodded earnestly. "Sure, Brody. Anything."

"Maddy tells me . . ." Brody paused, then continued in a voice that reflected genuine puzzlement, "that you two don't want to work together anymore."

Smitty was surprised at the depth of his own disappointment. He hadn't realized Violet was feeling the same way. The idea brought a vague ache to his chest. Sure, he'd figured some time apart might smooth out the tension between them, but suddenly the notion of not seeing her every day seemed worse than fighting all the time.

"Now, boss," he began, "let's not make any hasty decisions—"

But Brody rolled right over him, saying, "However, even if we get the funding, it'll be a while until the second boat puts out to sea. Also, I've been thinking that one of us should stay on land to coordinate the stranding rescue volunteers, organize the new educational programs we're going to run from the center, and help with the databases."

Ahab, another of Dolphin Friendly's intern-turned-researchers, had been working on a computer model of dolphin and whale strandings on the eastern seaboard. He didn't seem to mind spending long hours indoors clicking away at his computer, but Smitty would rather eat chum than be stuck on land, working inside the stranding center day after day after day. . . .

Stuck on land. Brody's planned punishment suddenly became crystal clear.

Violet was just as quick to put two and two together. "Now Brody, don't be hasty. You wouldn't want to pull one of your senior researchers out of the field. You need us."

"Exactly. I need both of you. But not when your minds are elsewhere. I need you with me—body and soul—and the dolphins do too." Brody reached across the chart table and plucked a key ring from the hook next to the ship-to-shore radio. "Take these."

Smitty did so, feeling a quiver of unease. As always, he hid it with a joke. "What are they? Keys to the convertible I always wanted?"

Brody snorted. "Not hardly. They belong to a twenty-foot refrigerator truck that you two," he glared at his friends, "are driving to Florida."

Seeing where this was going, Smitty tried to stop it before it happened. "But boss—"

"Nope." Brody shook his head. "My mind is made up. Take the keys or you're both on shore duty starting now."

"Brody—" Violet began.

"Nope. Neither one of you is going to talk me out of this." Their boss grinned and stretched before lacing his fingers together behind his head. "If you want to complain, talk to Maddy. This was her idea."

"No kidding," Smitty muttered, "Miss 'why can't we all get along' just had to get involved, didn't she?" But he wasn't really mad. Brody was right.

He and Violet had to make peace or stay away from each other for good. This half-friendship, half-enmity wasn't working for either of them, and it wasn't helping Dolphin Friendly.

"I don't get it. What are you talking about?" Violet demanded.

"We're talking about a road trip," Brody told her. "You and Mr. Smith here are taking a big, ugly refrigerated truck down to Florida to pick up a California sea lion named Jasper."

"A sea lion? In Florida?" Violet repeated, and Smitty felt almost sorry for her. "With *Smitty*?" The flush that climbed her cheeks was downright lovely, and her perfect nails clenched the edge of the chart table as if it were a lifeline. She looked utterly horrified.

He felt a thump of disappointment. Was the idea of spending a few days stuck in a vehicle with him really so awful? If so, friendship, or even a truce between them seemed unlikely.

"It was your idea, wasn't it, Violet?" Brody looked to Smitty for confirmation. "You suggested that we use a trained sea lion to cut the grand opening ribbon with oversized scissors, right?"

She nodded, then shook her head. "Yes, but I was kidding. I didn't think you'd actually go for it."

"Well, I thought it was a good idea. The politicians will love it. I asked a few people, and it turns out that Jasper the sea lion was already scheduled to be transferred from the Florida Stranding Rescue Seaquarium up to Boston. I got them to agree that if we drove him, Jasper could make a quick detour to the Cape on the way to his new home. The trainers have worked with him and a pair of foam rubber scissors, and now he's ready for transport."

"T-transport?" she stammered.

Smitty patted her shoulder, wishing she didn't look so upset by the idea of a road trip with him. "It won't be so bad, Vi."

She shrugged him off as though she couldn't stand his touch. Backing away from the chart table, she held up both hands. "No way. I'm not going."

Brody shook his head. "Sorry. Not an option. I

need my senior people in charge of this move and you two are it."

Smitty didn't bother to ask whether Ahab and Ishmael had been scheduled for the trip until the darned video camera landed in the drink. He'd bet on it.

"And if I refuse?" Violet asked.

"Then you're both on land duty as of tomorrow, and I'll tell Ahab to make you guide all the preschool field trips scheduled to tour the rescue center. When you're done with that, you'll be on data entry." Brody grimaced when they both shuddered in horror. "I'm not kidding. Do it. This may sound stupid, but Maddy thinks you two have some stuff to work out. I'm giving you three and a half days. Take a day or two to drive down, and then drive Jasper straight back for the ceremony. By the time you get home, I want you to have worked things out so you can at least be civil to each other."

Violet stuck out her chin, though her eyes were wary. "Or?"

Brody looked from the broken camera to her and back again. "Or you're no use to me as field researchers, either of you. As Maddy's parents learned, a boat is no place to make mistakes. I won't run the risk of you getting hurt because your minds aren't on your work. Figure it out, or you're on desk duty."

Brody stood, walked to the door, opened it, then

closed it softly behind him, probably figuring they'd like to get a head start on making up.

Brody always had been an optimist. Smitty would like nothing better than to make things right with Violet, but he wasn't even sure when it had gone wrong. He didn't have a clue how to start fixing their friendship.

So he went with sarcasm, dangling the keys off his index finger and grinning. "What do you say, Vi? Ready for a little fun in the sun?"

She glared at him. "I'll go on this trip. Under duress. But I won't make nice to you, no matter what he says." She stomped off, slamming the door for effect, but not before Smitty thought he glimpsed a sheen of moisture in her eyes.

It brought him up short. Violet never cried. If the thought of three days alone with him was enough to reduce her to tears, then things between them were worse than he thought.

Maybe Maddy had a point, after all. Maybe he and Violet *did* have some things to work out.

He just wished he knew where to start.

"Son of a lamprey thinks he's going to get one over on me, he's sadly mistaken," Violet muttered the next morning as she chucked a second pair of shorts into her overnight bag. "I'll go on Brody's stupid road trip, but I won't make nice to Smitty no matter how cute he thinks he is."

She pulled a couple of blouses from their hangers and tossed them on the ruffled bedspread. Then she rolled her eyes at the bed. She kept meaning to replace the ruffles with something less girly. Some days she barely noticed the frou-frou. Other days, like today, it grated on her nerves.

The room was decorated with lace, doilies, and other fluffy things she couldn't even name. When Maddy had closed the Smugglers Cove Inn and turned her grandparents' old B and B into the temporary headquarters of the Stranding Center, Violet had fully intended to strip her room of lace and frills and hang up a few of her favorite vintage movie posters.

She hadn't gotten around to it yet. There was always something more interesting to do, like head into the Cove's so-called downtown and shoot a game of pool at the diner, or take one of the Zodiacs out, kill the engine, and just drift for a while and watch the stars while she listened to the humpback whales sing.

The ocean. God, she loved the ocean.

"I can't believe he's threatening to ground me." She felt an itchy, prickling sensation behind her eyes and was shocked by the thought that she was close to tears. She hadn't really cried since grad school, and it wasn't an experience she was hoping to repeat anytime soon.

A noise at the door had her turning quickly away and scrubbing at her eyes with the blouse she held in her hands. It wouldn't do for one of the crew to see her red-eyed. She had an image to maintain.

But it wasn't one of the crew. Or at least Violet didn't see her that way. Not yet.

"Maddy." Violet kept her tone polite. Though her romance with Brody had died an uninteresting death long before Dolphin Friendly arrived in Smuggler's Cove, Violet couldn't help feeling hurt that Brody had found someone else. And married her.

It was a sad fact that men didn't marry Violet. They married the next girl they dated *after* Violet.

"Violet." Maddy's return greeting also bordered on cool, but she continued, "I came to see whether you need any help packing for your trip."

"Came to gloat, did you? Wanted to see how Brody's ex-girlfriend was taking her punishment?" Violet folded the blouses willy-nilly and pushed them into the bag. She knew she was being unkind, but Maddy's marriage into the group had changed dynamics that had been stable for nearly a decade, and Violet wasn't quite ready to forgive her for that.

Surprisingly, instead of denying the accusation, Maddy looked at her feet and twisted her fingers together. "I'd be lying if I said it didn't bother me that you and Brody once had a relationship, but I'd like to think I'm a better person than that."

The words *unlike you* hung between the women and Violet had to work to stop a quick grin.

Perhaps Maddy was ready to join the pecking order of Dolphin Friendly after all. She began to work up a reply that was snippy enough to keep the conversation going but not so nasty that she'd have to apologize, but then Maddy took the wind completely out of her sails, saying, "And this trip wasn't intended as punishment by any of us. More like enforced togetherness for you and Smitty. I care about both of you—"

Violet snickered, but she had to force it past a sudden lump in her throat.

Maddy shook her head. "No, it's true. Smitty has been wonderful to me all along. He's kind and funny and sensitive—"

"A real prince," Violet murmured, earning a warning look that made her feel mean.

"He is, though, and you know it. You just don't want to admit it. And then there's you."

Violet waited, curious what positive thing Maddy would find to say about her. There couldn't be much. She hadn't been at her best lately. The changes within Dolphin Friendly had unsettled her. Brody's marriage had removed him from the triangle of friends and put her in closer contact with Smitty.

Contact that made her yearn for things that could never work.

"You've been a member of Dolphin Friendly since the beginning. Sure, you're prickly," Maddy said, and Violet grinned at the description. She'd worked long and hard to earn it, because it made the men take her seriously. She might be five-foot-nothing, but she held her own. Maddy continued, "But you're also the best underwater photographer I've seen in a long while, your sonar and acoustic skills are second to none, and you're the only person on the boat who can beat Ishmael at taxonomy." Maddy paused and touched her hair, which was less of a frizzy mess now that she was using the right conditioner. "And you helped me with my hair, even if you don't want anyone to know about it."

"Why do I get the feeling there's a 'but' coming up next?" Violet abandoned her packing and ran a piece of clothing between her fingers while she stared at Maddy. She'd never been entirely comfortable with 'girl talk,' but she couldn't quite bring herself to end the conversation. It was starting to get interesting.

"Not so much a 'but.' More like an observation." Maddy twisted her fingers again as if unsure how Violet would react. "I don't think you're happy."

Violet snorted even as her shoulders did that tense, tightening thing they'd been doing more often lately. "What's not to be happy about? I love my work; you said yourself I'm good at it. We've gotten half our grant, the stranding center opens in a week, and we should get the other half of the money. In the time we've stayed in Smugglers Cove I've dived with more marine mammals than I've seen since we left Monterey Bay." She looked around the room, trying to think of another reason she was happy. "And I've finally got my own closet," she finished, waving at the room.

Oddly enough, she realized it was true. She loved her closet. And part of her was happy, for all the reasons she'd mentioned, including the closet.

Personal space had been in short supply on *Streaker*, and until they had taken up residence in the Smugglers Cove Inn, the crew had lived out of suitcases and rented rooms. Violet enjoyed knowing she was coming back to the same bed after each trip and it didn't even bother her anymore that she had Maddy to thank for it.

It shouldn't matter that Smitty slept just down the hall. It *wouldn't* matter, she assured herself, because there was nothing more than friendship between them, and sometimes not even that.

Maddy flashed a smile. The inn had belonged to

her grandparents and she was justifiably proud of it. "I'm glad you like the closet. However, Brody and I feel that neither you nor Smitty are happy right now with the current state of affairs."

Was it Violet's imagination, or had Maddy stressed the last word?

"Have you—" Violet paused and swallowed, hating herself for needing to know. "Have you asked Smitty about it?"

Maddy wrinkled her nose. "Yes. He just told a joke and changed the subject."

"Typical," Violet muttered, hastening to add, "not that there's anything he should have told you, of course. We just get on each other's nerves. That's all."

"Of course," Maddy replied, reaching to take a blouse out of the carryall and refold it more neatly. "That's all. Which is why you've packed the shirt he complimented you on a few days ago and the bikini that nearly made his eyes cross when you wore it last week."

"Not intentionally." Violet made a grab for the offending items but Maddy held on. The women indulged in a brief tug-of-war over the miniscule bikini top, which was nothing more than a pair of Band-Aid sized scraps of fabric held together with electric blue string, until Maddy gave up and sat down on the bed, laughing.

"Oh never mind. You don't have to tell me. But really Violet, just between us girls, don't you think he's even a little handsome?"

The phrase *just between us girls* took Violet aback. She didn't remember it ever being "us girls" before. A tomboy raised by three brothers, she considered herself eminently qualified to deal with men, but was at a loss when confronted by women—particularly friendly, emotionally open ones. So she deliberately misunderstood the question, hoping to fend off Maddy's good intentions. "Who, Brody?"

The other woman winced and held up a hand, "Please. Let's not talk about your past with my husband while I'm feeling a brief moment of bonhomie here. You know very well who I'm talking about."

Zipping her bag shut, Violet shrugged. "Sure, Smitty's cute enough. When he's not being annoying, which is almost never." She lifted the bag, glanced at Maddy, and ignored the urge to beg, *please don't make me go on this trip.* "Guess I'm all packed."

"I'll go see if Smitty's ready." Maddy headed for the door, turning when Violet called her back. "Yes?"

"I, uh—" Violet cleared her throat. "I was thinking that maybe after the grand opening, you and I could go out sometime."

"Out?" Maddy's voice almost squeaked on the word. "You and me?"

Violet shrugged uncomfortably. "Yeah. I want new curtains, maybe a bedspread, and some . . . decorations or something. I thought with you running the inn for so long, you'd know the best places to go. . . ."

Maddy's pleased smile was answer enough, as was her quick wash of color. "It's a date. We'll do it when you come back from your trip."

Both women's eyes were drawn to the window at the sound of a large, off-tune truck pulling into the clamshell driveway.

The horn beeped obnoxiously and Smitty hollered, "Truck's here, Vi! Hurry up and let's get going. We've got a sea lion to chauffeur and a deadline to meet!"

Violet rolled her eyes and shouldered her overnight bag. "Yeah, we'll do it when I get back. That is, if I'm not in jail for murder or something."

As she left the room, Violet thought she heard Maddy murmur, "Or something. . . ."

Chapter Three

"It's about time, I was getting ready to leave without you." As the truck idled in the driveway of Maddy's inn, Smitty danced his feet over the gas and the clutch, winding the refrigerator truck's engine up to drown out the first part of Violet's response as she hiked herself into the high passenger seat and slammed the door.

"—and another thing!" She paused when he just laughed and tapped on the gas again. "Oh, never mind."

There was no backseat and the stick shift took up most of the middle, so she had to tuck her bag next to her feet. She squirmed around and kicked at the clutter until everything was where she wanted it, and Smitty had to force himself to look away from her legs, which seemed to go on for miles. There were days he could make himself ignore her legs. Then there were days like today.

The idea of spending the next few days sharing the tiny truck cab with her was disturbing, and not because he disliked her. More because he didn't. Not really.

"Here, this is for you two." Ishmael and Ahab—one of them was actually named Peter, but Smitty could never remember which one—stood next to the truck with an empty specimen jar.

"My parents always used a pickle jar when we road tripped as a family. I thought this would do." Ishmael leaned across Smitty and placed the jar on the dashboard. The label on it read *"Pay to fight, make up for free."*

Ahab nodded. "The rule is that whichever of you starts the fight has to put five bucks in the jar. At the end of the trip you take the money and go out for a nice dinner, where you make up for every nasty thing you said on the road."

Smitty looked at the jar and imagined it bursting with fives, tens, and twenties by the time they passed the Maryland border headed south. His lips stretched into a smile.

"Huh. We'll be able to take ourselves off on a short cruise, never mind dinner," Violet said, paralleling his thoughts like she used to do.

He was relieved to see she was grinning. When she'd first come out of the house, she'd looked like she was walking to her own execution. It bothered him to think she was dreading their trip. Once upon a time, they would have loved just such a getaway.

Once upon a time.

"Oh, good." Brody approached the truck with his arm slung across his wife's shoulders. "The boys gave you their present. Great idea, isn't it?" Maddy looked up at her husband with a smile, and Smitty felt a quick jab under his heart at the sight of two people he loved so obviously in love with each other. Watching them fall for each other had reminded him of emotions long buried. Opportunities long missed.

He glanced over at Violet, but she hadn't noticed the exchange. She was too busy rummaging in her "purse," a faded green canvas bag that had contained at various times everything from an oil-slicked herring gull to a diamond tiara donated for Dolphin Friendly's annual charity auction.

"I think you're just sending us off so you can make some time with that pretty lady there." He grinned and gestured from Brody to Maddy. "If I'm not around, you won't have any competition, will you, boss?" He turned with a mock warning to the two younger members of the team. "Ishmael, Ahab, better watch out, he'll be sending you off on some trumped-up errand next, just so he can have some time alone with his wife."

Ahab shook his head. "Oh, no sir. We're taking *Streaker* out to recount the harbor seal pups at the rookery off the Point."

Brody's self-satisfied smile was confirmation enough that he'd planned the distraction. It had taken the three senior members of the team a full day to be sure of the original count. It might take the junior scientists twice that.

"Okay, here it is," Violet announced, pulling her wallet out of the disreputable green bag. She selected two twenty-dollar bills and folded them neatly before leaning across the stick shift and reaching for the jar on the dash.

She was wearing a shirt that Smitty was particularly fond of, a lightly ribbed tank that clung to her torso and left her strong shoulders and arms bare. One of those arms brushed against his hand as she stretched across the truck. His muscles clenched and his foot depressed the gas pedal, causing the engine to race higher. If he moved just an inch, he could touch the bare skin of her shoulder. If he rotated his hand just a bit, he could trail his finger down the back of her neck, and then—

And then what? If she'd wanted him that way, she would have married him when he'd asked her back in grad school. She'd turned him down back then because she hadn't wanted him enough. Why would things be any different now?

The engine slowed down as his foot lifted. He consciously unclenched his jaw. She pulled the specimen jar over to her side of the truck, unscrewed the lid and dropped the forty dollars inside before returning the jar to the dash.

"What's that?" Maddy asked with merriment dancing in her eyes. "An apology for past fights?"

"Ha!" Violet snickered. "No way." She grinned wickedly and Smitty felt an answering grin touch his lips when she said, "That's a down payment on things to come!"

She leaned back in her seat, slid on a pair of dark sunglasses, and crossed her perfect legs. "Drive on then, Mr. Smith. We have miles to go before we sleep."

She soon contradicted herself by nodding off before they'd passed over the Cape Cod Canal.

Violet dreamed of water. Ever since she was a little girl, she'd dreamed of water—of being in water, flying over it, or walking next to it while the sun set and the sky turned pink and an auburn-haired grad student held her hand.

"What did you think of Prof. Murphy's questions on oceanic convection cells, Vi?" He let go of her hand, crouched down, and pulled a pink spiral shell from the sand. "Here, it's as pretty as you are."

Violet, fresh from the Midwest and unused to boys other than her brothers and cousins, blushed and took the shell. "I thought the questions were fair enough, but they were probably easier for people like you who grew up near the water. Until I came out here for school, I'd never even seen the ocean."

Except in my dreams.

Smitty shrugged, took her hand again, and squeezed it. She felt the contact all the way up her arm. "Yeah, but you're better at the theoretical stuff than I am. I bet it comes from having to argue your way through a large family."

He left her, picked up a few rocks, and tossed them in the water. His mother had died just that summer, leaving him alone in the world. He'd told her about it once, but it wasn't a subject he liked discussing.

She knew he envied her the big, sprawling Oliver clan she'd come from. In a way, she hadn't appreciated her extended family until she left for the marine sciences program at U.C. Santa Cruz. She didn't miss them so much anymore, but the little bit that Smitty had told her of his own childhood made her realize that a large extended family might not be the burden she'd always thought.

So she dared to step in close to him and slide an arm around his waist like she'd wanted to do since they'd started hanging out together on the first day of orientation. She gave him a little squeeze and relished the warm muscles beneath her hand. "I think what's important is what you learn from how you grow up. I didn't realize it before, but having so many relatives around was a good thing. I won't go back home to live—it's too far from the sea—but I like knowing they're there if I need them."

He tipped his head toward her. "Sounds nice. You going to have a big family of your own so your kids will grow up with what you had?"

Violet shrugged. She was twenty-two and hardly ready to consider that sort of thing. She'd think about children later, once she had her career firmly established. She wanted to work with marine mammals. Maybe manatees. Then perhaps she and her husband would talk about starting a family. "I guess. Someday."

She felt Smitty's arm slide around her shoulders and loved the warmth of it, and the huskiness in his voice when he whispered, "Me too, Vi. Me too."

And the world shook convulsively.

"What the—?" Violet swore as the truck jolted again and her head smacked against the window. She grabbed for the door handle and hauled herself up-right as the truck bucked like a frantic porpoise. "What's wrong?"

Smitty hung on to the steering wheel with one hand and downshifted with the other, muttering about air brakes, bald tires, and grooved pavement. "Sorry to interrupt your nap, but Interstate 95 seems to be under spontaneous construction."

Violet glanced out the window that still bore the imprint of her face. Great, she'd been drooling in her sleep. How attractive.

Jersey barriers and orange barrels zipped past the window, slowing now that the truck was coming back under Smitty's control. The road in front of them was grooved and torn up. No wonder she'd been beaten back to consciousness. They were lucky they hadn't blown a tire, coming on such road conditions without warning.

Life was simply easier on the ocean. No roads. No construction.

No detours.

She glanced over at Smitty again. His face had relaxed back into its familiar lines now that the immediate crisis had passed, and she couldn't help seeing the boy she'd been dreaming about in the man sitting beside her. Couldn't help wishing things had been different.

Stupid, she chided herself. *Don't be stupid.*

Feeling unaccountably raw, she aimed low. "There's no such thing as spontaneous construction. I'm sure you've been passing signs for miles that warned drivers like you not to speed through the construction zone." Then another thought struck. Her voice sharpened. "And why are we on I-95? The Pike's quicker, or even I-84."

"Not on a weekday and not coming from Smugglers Cove." Smitty's fingers tightened on the steering wheel and she could see a muscle in his jaw tick. Like most men she'd known, Smitty always thought he knew the best set of directions, and woe to the woman—usually Violet—who dared challenge them.

"But there's always construction on 95 and it meanders all along the coast. It's going to take forever to get through New York City, and by then we'll hit lunchtime traffic."

Violet enjoyed the way his eyes went dark when his temper rose. She loved the feeling of blood humming just beneath her skin when their anger started to crackle. She wondered which one of them would owe five bucks for the battle she felt brewing. Then she decided she didn't care. She'd put forty dollars in the jar. She was fighting on account.

And arguing with Smitty had become one of her

favorite pastimes. At least when they were fighting, she knew he was paying attention to her.

"Well if my *copilot* hadn't snored her way across Rhode Island and into Connecticut, we wouldn't be having this conversation, would we?" They were bumping slowly along the ruined road now, stuck behind an overloaded truck that was laboring to climb the hill ahead.

"I don't snore," Violet said, offended. Okay, maybe she'd drooled, but she certainly hadn't snored.

"If you say so, Vi." He sighed and rubbed the back of his neck. "You ready for a snack and a gas break?" Clearly tired of the conversation and the traffic, Smitty took the next off ramp and pulled into the optimistically named Lovely Truck Stop.

It was anything but lovely. But then again, anything short of the open ocean left much to be desired in Violet's opinion.

"Sure. Whatever." She flipped the visor down to check how badly her nap had messed with her hair. Then she frowned. No mirror. What kind of a vehicle was this, anyway?

She ignored Smitty's eye roll and hopped out of the truck as soon as it stopped. "See ya inside."

If she played her cards right, Violet figured she could avoid pumping gas the whole way to Florida and back. She didn't mind fueling up *Streaker* or any of the other boats, but something about working with cars bugged her. She was a sea creature through and through, which was why there was no way she was letting Brody demote her to land duty. Even if it meant being nice to Smitty for the next few days.

And who knew? Maybe they'd even have some fun on the way.

She bought sodas and snacks for the two of them, grabbing Smitty's favorite sticky buns and chips along with pretzels and peppermints for herself. Figuring the caffeine would be a welcome jolt—they'd probably drive through till dark and stop somewhere in Virginia—she ordered a pair of coffees and added the fake sweetener and low-fat milk she knew he preferred—though why he used diet products she'd never understand. His body was perfect.

Not that she noticed such things, of course.

They passed each other in the parking lot and she tried to ignore the fact that he looked extra handsome with his shirtsleeves rolled up to his elbows and his pants wrinkled slightly at the knees and cuffs.

Maybe there was a touch of sentiment left in her mind from that dream, or maybe it was seeing him out of their shared element, but it struck her just how many years they'd known each other.

And just how much she'd loved that red-haired young man who'd walked with her on the beaches of Monterey.

"Everything okay?" He took the coffee from her and drank deep, sighing his appreciation. When she didn't answer, he cocked a brow. "Vi?"

She shook herself mentally. That was a long time ago. Lots of water had passed beneath each of their keels since he'd been that boy. Since she'd been that green, naïve girl.

Since he'd turned from her to marry Ellen, and then after his divorce had welcomed her back into his life with nothing more than a pat on the shoulder.

Smitty touched her arm where it was wrapped around the bag of snacks. She realized she was clutching the chips hard enough to grind them to dust. "What's wrong?" he asked in concern.

Jumping at the sting of the contact, she almost spilled her coffee. She used the move to place her arm out of his reach. "Nothing's wrong. I'll see you back at the truck." She spun on her heel and marched back to the ugly box truck.

And wondered why, for the second time that day, she felt like crying.

Smitty watched her go and wished he knew what he'd done this time to upset her.

Wished he knew how to fix it.

Shaking his head, he walked into the truck stop to pay for the gas. The next few days were going to be difficult, just like the last few months had been. He didn't know how much longer he was going to be able to stand by and watch Violet mourn her lost relationship with Brody.

He hadn't thought it was serious when his two best friends dated a few years ago. At least he'd convinced himself they weren't serious, because as much as he tried to hide it, the alternative bothered him. He'd wanted to ask Violet out when she'd returned to the group after her internship in Seattle, but the memory of his spurned proposal had held him back. She hadn't wanted to marry him in grad school, so why would he think she'd want him two years later?

Then she and Brody had started dating, and it hadn't been an option. Smitty didn't poach on his best friend's girl.

When Brody and Violet had broken up, it had barely caused a ripple in Dolphin Friendly, and Smitty had been relieved. Still, he hadn't found the guts to ask her out. Instead, he'd gotten her attention by sewing her into her hammock and sounding the alarms.

It had been one of his finer moments, and it had begun a new facet of their relationship. Perhaps they couldn't be a couple, Smitty had reasoned, but at least they could be friends. They had existed in an unsteady, practical joke–filled truce ever since.

Since Brody's wedding, though, Violet's temper had grown steadily worse. Smitty knew her well enough to know that she used anger to beat back other emotions. The best he could figure, she was upset that Brody had married Maddy. And the thought annoyed him.

Frowning now, he stepped up to the gas window. "Paying for pump six."

"That it?" asked the pretty blond locked inside the bulletproof compartment. He nodded and pushed his company card through the slot. Glancing past the plate glass window, he saw a gleaming convertible next to the refrigerator truck. A tall, dark-haired man was leaning against the front of the expensive sports car, talking to Violet. He grinned, and perfect teeth flashed.

Violet smiled back at him.

Smitty clenched his jaw and signed the slip hard enough to tear the carbon paper.

He crossed the parking lot just in time to hear her laughter ring out across the tarmac. He paused. When was the last time he'd heard Violet laugh? Really laugh? Not the brittle chuckle that signaled a practical joke gone well, but the carefree, young sound she was making now?

He wasn't sure, but it seemed like it had been a long time. Maybe Brody was right. Maybe they all needed a change. However, he thought, narrowing his eyes, that change didn't need to include some roadside hustler in a sports car.

Planning to dispatch the guy in short order, Smitty scowled as he walked up behind Violet and draped an arm around her shoulders. "Ready to hit the road, babe?" He glared at Mr. Convertible, who got the hint right away and backed off even before Smitty cocked an eyebrow and said, "We have lots of driving to do before bedtime."

When the sports car had departed in a swirl of expensive fumes, Violet turned on him. Her eyes glowed with temper and she poked him in the chest, just above his heart.

"Just who do you think you are? I was talking to him about the stranding center. You know . . . donations? Besides, we have plenty of time to get the sea lion back up to Cape Cod, and Brody said we should enjoy ourselves on the way down, didn't he?" She was toe to toe with him, ready to do battle. "So what was that little act all about?"

Smitty gritted his teeth. She was right, he'd overreacted. But he hadn't liked the way Mr. Convertible had been looking at her, and he'd liked the direction of his thoughts even less. "I don't think Brody was suggesting that we pick up men at a truck stop in Connecticut, do you? I think he expected us to get to Florida and make nice with the Seaquarium folks. That's the kind of contact Dolphin Friendly needs right now."

"Well, it's not the kind of contact *I* need," Violet grumped, and Smitty cringed to think what kind of contact she'd been looking for from Mr. Convertible. A slick guy like that would never be good enough for her.

He held up both hands in surrender. "Well, I can't help you there, Vi."

And, surprisingly, she got even madder at that. But it wasn't the loud, exciting, pretty anger Smitty loved so much. It was a quieter, sadder anger that made him feel like he should apologize for something. Her shoulders slumped. "Yeah, you've made that more than clear. You can't give me what I need. Don't worry—I figured that out when you married Ellen."

She climbed into the truck, taking the driver's side, and slammed the door.

Though Smitty tried to start several conversations—and one fight—Violet made it clear she didn't want to talk through the rest of the afternoon and into the early evening. The miles rolled beneath the refrigerator truck's wheels, and they passed from country to city and back again, the temperature warming as they slid southward.

By the time they stopped at dusk, Smitty was tired of silence and his own confused emotions. Had she been trying to tell him that she wanted a relationship after all? He wasn't sure, and he was tired of trying to figure it out. He was tired of the truck and tired of being in the same clothes. He was hungry and cranky and inexplicably tense from having spent the last hundred miles staring at Violet's hands on the steering wheel.

He'd seen those hands just about every day for the past eight years, ever since she'd rejoined Dolphin Friendly after her stint in Seattle. He'd seen those hands soothe a seal tangled in fishing nets. He'd seen them push a stranded dolphin back to sea, and he'd seen them fly like fury over the computer keyboards back on *Streaker*. And he realized as he watched her drive that he'd never seen the perfect oval nails unpolished.

Such a small thing, but it reflected her personality so well. Nothing undone. Nothing out of place.

"How often do you paint your fingernails, Vi?" he asked as they dragged their duffels out of the truck and into the generic lobby of the generic just-off-the-highway hotel.

She glanced at him, then away. "We've been driving since this morning and that's the best conversational gambit you can come up with? Pretty weak,

Smitty." She signed the register and grabbed her key. "And I'm out of here. I'll see you in the morning."

He stopped her. "Vi? Don't you want to grab some dinner or something? Maybe go for a swim?"

Even as he made the invitation, it felt strange. They ate together and swam together seven days a week, but never alone. There was always someone else around, either joining in or passing through. That was what Dolphin Friendly was all about. Or least it had been, before Brody and Maddy's marriage.

Violet shrugged and faked a yawn. "I don't think so. I'm just going to crash. See you tomorrow." She disappeared up the stairs.

Smitty got his own room and changed into his swimming trunks. He called the front desk and ordered room service to be sent up to Violet, knowing that she'd forget to eat if there wasn't food in front of her. Then he went down to swim.

He was twitchy from all the driving and needed to burn some calories. That's all it was, he told himself—too much energy.

His restlessness had nothing to do with the woman down the hall.

Chapter Four

"Where are you?" Brody's voice on the cell phone was as clear as if he were sitting next to her. Violet glanced at the driver's side and wished for a fleeting moment that Brody *was* the one sitting next to her. His presence never bothered her the way Smitty's presence did.

Which is probably why her and Brody's relationship had died of boredom.

"Somewhere in South Carolina," she answered. "We're making pretty good time." Mostly because there hadn't been much conversation. Smitty was driving like he wanted to get the trip over with as soon as possible, and she couldn't blame him. It wasn't his fault she hadn't slept well the night before, but she'd snapped at him first thing that morning anyway.

Well, technically it *was* his fault she had tossed and turned through the night, ending up staring at the ceiling, angry and frustrated that she kept remembering scenes of their time together at U.C. Santa Cruz. She was remembering things they had shared B.E.—Before Ellen.

"So you'll reach the Seaquarium sometime tomorrow?" Brody's voice was familiar and settled her jangled nerves. He continued, "Remember, Jasper won't be ready for transport until the day after tomorrow, so don't feel like you have to rush down there. You'll have to hurry home, though, to be back in time for the opening ceremonies."

Violet assured him that they had everything under control and finished the call. When she'd returned her phone to the ugly green bag she kept meaning to replace, she realized the truck was slowing.

"Want to switch drivers?" She made her voice as pleasant as she knew how, hoping Smitty would take it as an apology for her attitude that morning. She wondered whether it would lighten things between them if she tried a practical joke. Then she decided that with her recent luck with practical jokes, she'd probably try to give him a hotfoot and accidentally blow up the truck. If that happened, she'd be on land duty for the rest of her natural life.

Smitty guided the big box truck down an off ramp and turned down a side street, following a series of big blue arrows. "No. We're stopping here. Brody said there was no hurry, right?"

"Yes, but. . . ."

"No buts. We've made great time and we've been working our tails off the last few months at the stranding center. Let's take a break for a couple of hours. What do you say?" He waved at the colorful latticework of slides and tubes, at the enormous sign they were parked under.

Water World.

Violet felt her heart turn over. It could've been another sign, at another park on the opposite side of the country—a decade in their past.

She shook her head. "Smitty, I don't think. . . ."

He touched her hand gently. "You used to love these places, Vi. Don't let what happened back then take that away from you." He tried for a light tone. "I promise I won't ask you to marry me this time."

The words were wistful, the memory bittersweet. Violet pushed it aside and found a hint of the anger she'd carried for the past decade. "Somehow, I don't remember you asking me to marry you in the first place. It was more like 'I don't want to be alone. Let's make a family.' "

The engine idled roughly and a pair of children on their way to the entrance of the water park glanced curiously at the refrigerator truck as their parents tugged them past.

"It's the same thing," he said, sounding surprised.

Violet shook her head. "Not to me it wasn't, and not to you either or you wouldn't have replaced me so easily. Ellen wanted to be a family. I didn't. Your choice seemed simple." She sighed and reached for the door handle, then forced false cheer into her voice. "But why rehash all this now? It was a long time ago and a lot of water under each of our bridges."

She hopped out of the truck and turned to rummage through her squashed bag for her bathing suit— what there was of it.

"Wait a second! That's not fair. You turned me down!" He was out of the truck in an instant, coming around to her side practically radiating shock and indignation.

"Yes, I did. And beyond that, I don't really want to talk about it, do you? It's ancient history, Smitty. Let's leave it in the past." Determinedly, she pushed the sadness back into the corner of her mind where it belonged. "And you're right. We deserve a break. Let's hit the water park and see if we still remember how it's done."

She looked up to see if he was with her and found his eyes glued to the bikini. She dangled one of the tiny straps off a finger. "You with me?"

He swallowed. "Um. Yeah."

Though a faint sadness echoed in her chest, Violet grinned, grabbed a towel, and sashayed towards the entrance of the park. She had, she realized, spent so much time recently being mean to him that she'd forgotten how much fun they'd once had together. And how good it felt when the thought of seeing her in that bikini could make his eyes bug out, even though it had been ten years since they'd been anything more than friends.

Ten long years during which he'd been married and divorced, and she'd not . . . been married.

The water park had been his idea, but as he watched Violet disappear into the ladies' changing room, Smitty wished he'd pulled over at a petting zoo instead. Even a flea market or a country fair would've been easier than this.

It hadn't been until he'd pulled into the water park and set the brake that he realized that he'd brought them back to the place where it had all gone wrong. Until that day at California's WaveForm Water Park, he'd truly believed that he and Violet were going to spend the rest of their lives together. He'd truly believed they were soul mates.

He'd been so lost when classes began that year at U.C. Santa Cruz. His mother's death had set him adrift in the world without any family and only a few close friends. Then he'd met Violet at orientation. She'd been smart, sassy, beautiful . . . and seemed just as alone as he'd felt.

They'd become friends, then a couple. And the more he'd learned about her sprawling, loving family in the middle of the country, the more Smitty had envied it. The more he'd wanted those kinds of roots, that kind of commitment.

He'd thought she wanted it too.

"You're not changed yet!"

He blinked back from the past. And blinked again. The tiny blue bikini danced before his eyes, partially hidden by a clever wrap that she'd tied across her hips.

"Smitty? You okay?"

He swallowed and nodded, trapped somewhere between the past and a fantasy. "Fine. I'll just. . . ." He gestured towards the changing rooms. "Be right back."

He needed a minute alone. The past and the present were too tangled up in his head. And thoughts of the future? They were just as tangled. It seemed obvious they couldn't keep on fighting the way they'd been doing lately, but he didn't see how they could be something as simple as friends. And if not friends, then what? He didn't like the idea of not seeing her on a daily basis, but the alternative was impossible.

Sighing, he shook his head and went to change into his trunks.

By the time he caught up with her at one of the monstrous water rides, Smitty had his thoughts back under control. He and Violet were coworkers, nothing more. They'd tried the other before, and she'd made it painfully clear that they weren't looking for the same things out of life. So they'd have some fun at the water park, get the rattling box truck back on the road, and reach Florida sometime the next day. They'd pick up Jasper, drive like heck to get home before either the sea lion overheated or they killed each other, and find some way to convince Brody that they were friends again.

Simple.

"Oh good, you're here. I've saved you a place." Violet grabbed his hand and swung him into the line just as the family in front of them was buckled into a fake log and sent on their way. Smitty noticed that there weren't seats in the logs—the riders were jammed in together, strapped down and expected to hold on for dear life.

He heard screaming from the other side of the ride, and a big splash.

"Our turn!" Violet pushed him towards a bobbing log. The attendant helped him sit in the soggy hollow, then gestured to Violet to sit in front.

"Put your arms around your girlfriend and hold on tight," the attendant chirped, and Violet backpedaled.

"Oh, I didn't realize—" The rest of her statement was lost when the attendant deftly shoved her into the log, tightened the belt across her hips, and sent them on their way.

At first, Violet held herself stiffly away from him, and Smitty smiled grimly when the first series of bumps and dips earned him an elbow in the ribs. "Vi, you might want to lean back against me. I don't bite, honest."

Then the fake log was picked up by a clanking track that lifted them high into the sky and they both forgot that they were feeling awkward with each other and started pointing at the other rides they could see from their new vantage point.

"Look over there! Let's hit the wave tank next." Violet grabbed his knee and pointed to a huge body of water. As they watched, a ten-foot-high swell started at one end and sped to the other, carrying swimmers and bodysurfers with it. Squeals of delight floated up to them, carrying over the rush of water and the clank of machinery.

And still the fake log was carried into the sky.

Short jets of water pumped over them and Violet squealed as she took a blast in the face. Then they were at the top of the enormous hill. The little log teetered a moment and she pressed back against Smitty as a rush of water pushed them over and down.

He felt the fake log lunge forward and freefall towards the ground, felt Violet's back mold itself to his front, and he wrapped his arms around her as they fell.

Then they were laughing and screaming and the water was coming at them from all sides, and as the fake log plunged into an enormous tank and raised a splash that seemed a mile high, Smitty reached for the sky—*look Ma, no hands!*—and felt ten years fall from his shoulders like they'd never passed.

They didn't make it to the wave tank right away, though Violet was itching to try it. The one thing she disliked about being based on Cape Cod was the lack of decent surfing. The Atlantic was okay, if you liked that sort of wave. And the Cape's North Shore even got decent rollers after a storm, but it didn't come close to the California beaches where she'd learned to surf.

As they bobbed down an artificial river that wound around the perimeter of the park, relaxing in separate black rubber tubes, Violet glanced over and wondered whether Smitty ever thought about the time he'd taught her to surf. Then she ground her teeth, annoyed that the only things she could seem to think about were things that had happened between two dumb kids at U.C. Santa Cruz.

She and Smitty weren't those kids anymore. They were grown-ups, well-respected researchers. Co-workers. A lot had happened since that long-ago day at a California water park.

Smitty had been married and divorced. Violet had spent the two years following Smitty's marriage studying killer whales in Puget Sound. After his divorce, she had rejoined Dolphin Friendly and the group had prospered. Each year, they had landed more interesting, more lucrative grants, seen more marine mammals, and rescued more stranded animals. Everything had been great. Then Brody had married Maddy.

And everything had changed.

It wasn't that she wanted Brody for herself—their brief relationship had been a big snore because they knew each other too well—but his marriage had been a shock to the trio of friends.

After Smitty's marriage failed and Violet rejoined the group without any rekindling of their romance, it had seemed obvious to her that marine researchers just weren't cut out for marriage. They were on the water too many months out of the year, and cared more for the ocean than they did for most people.

The founding members of Dolphin Friendly were all single, and they liked it that way. Or did they?

Standing on the sidelines while Brody and Maddy recited their vows, Violet had felt an unexpected and unwelcome tug. She'd wanted a family once. Maybe not as much or as quickly as Smitty had wanted one, which had been the big stumbling block between them, but she'd wanted kids. Wanted a husband who cared if she came home from sea every now and then. She rarely saw her own family anymore, and when she did, they asked careful questions and "tsked" when she said she didn't have anyone and grand-children weren't in the forecast.

She'd glanced at Smitty and thought she saw her own regrets mirrored in his face. She had wondered whether he would someday marry again and once again leave her the odd man out in Dolphin Friendly.

The next day—when Brody and Maddy were off on their extended honeymoon—she had filled Smitty's diving duffel with shaving cream. And the battles had begun.

"What're you thinking about, Vi?"

She looked over and saw that Smitty's rubber tube had drifted close to hers. His hair was wet, darkening his sun-bleached highlights to a rich chestnut. He pushed her tube ever so gently, making her spin. She let her head fall back and felt her hair dip in the water. Felt the familiar liquid surround her. God, she loved the water. The coolness caressed her scalp and made her think of being under the ocean. In every image in her mind's eye, Smitty was diving at her side.

And suddenly she wanted to tell him what she was thinking. She wanted to know whether he felt the same way about Brody and Maddy, whether he ever wondered what it would have been like if he'd waited for her rather than running off with Ellen two weeks after that fateful day at the water park.

She wanted to know if he ever thought of her that way now.

"Vi? Mackerel for your thoughts."

It was an old private joke.

"I was thinking of Brody and Maddy's wedding . . ." she began, then paused to gather her thoughts, struck by sudden indecision. What if he didn't feel the way she did? What if he hadn't noticed the way things had changed within Dolphin Friendly? What if he didn't care?

But she didn't get a chance to continue. Smitty's face twisted and his eyes shut once, as though he were in pain. "Oh. Yeah, right. Brody."

With a lurch, he slid off his inner tube and grabbed hers as well, dragging her into the shallow side of the lazy river, over to where a cluster of signs pointed to the next group of rides. He asked, "Ready for the Tidal Wave?" and boosted her onto dry land before she could answer.

"I—" *Not really,* she wanted to say. *I wanted to talk to you about Brody and Maddy. About us. About Dolphin Friendly. About why we always fight and what we could maybe do to change it.*

And it was then that Violet realized why she absolutely, positively could not voice the crazy feelings that had started creeping up on her just after that wedding. Why there was no way she and Smitty could try to pick up where they'd left off ten years ago.

She couldn't tell him any of it, because if they tried their relationship again and it crashed and burned, she'd have lost his friendship for good. She didn't think she could stand it if that happened.

So she gave him her best evil look and said, "I was *born* ready. Let's catch some waves," then turned away before he could say anything else.

The Tidal Wave was fun enough, but Smitty couldn't shake the feeling that Violet was determined to enjoy herself—come hell or high water—literally.

She grinned maniacally when the water level dropped to its lowest point and came crashing back into the tank, sending hundreds of wave riders hurtling a quarter mile or so on its crest. She laughed with the teenagers who treaded water near her, jostling for position and arguing which one of them should get to ride with the pretty lady in the tiny bikini.

But it was that sad, brittle laugh Smitty hated. He recognized it because that was the sound she'd been making more often than not of late.

It shouldn't have bothered him that she'd been thinking of Brody as they floated along. He knew there were unresolved issues between his two best friends. But he'd been nurturing the faint hope that she was enjoying herself, or that she was thinking fondly of that long-ago water park and those two young kids who hadn't loved each other quite enough.

Then again, why should she think of those times? They clearly hadn't meant as much to her as they had to him. She'd proven that when she'd turned him down. But something she'd said earlier bothered him—that he hadn't wanted her, he'd wanted a family.

Well really, what was the difference? As far as he'd been concerned back then, Violet *was* his family.

And in a way, she still was. She and Brody, and now Maddy, had become Smitty's family. Dolphin Friendly and his pet catfish Dusty were the sum of his worldly connections.

He couldn't regret the end of his marriage to Ellen, though he regretted that his constant absences had hurt her enough to drive her away. But he did feel a sort of hollow sadness that he was in his thirties, single and childless, and looking to stay that way for the foreseeable future. He had learned the hard way that marriages between landlubbers and marine researchers were destined for failure from the outset.

"Smitty! Look out, aaaah!" The water surged around him and Violet hurtled past as she caught a wave that he had missed.

He watched her surf away from him. And wished he'd caught the wave that had carried her away from him ten years earlier.

When she landed on shore, turned, and waved to him, Smitty shook his head and started to paddle.

Maybe this time he could catch her. And keep her.

Then again, maybe not.

Chapter Five

By late afternoon Violet had been splashed, dunked, doused, whistled at, and for a very brief moment had been in danger of parting company with her bikini top. She was tired, waterlogged, and supremely happy. Or she would have been, if it hadn't been for Smitty's rotten mood.

They were sitting under a cheerful striped umbrella sipping sodas and munching on a shared nacho plate. Well, Violet was munching and sipping. Smitty was glaring at his straw.

"What's your problem?" she finally asked. He'd been grumpy since they left the Tidal Wave, or maybe a bit before. She wondered whether it had anything to do with their aborted conversation in the lazy river. Maybe he was worried about the changes happening in Dolphin Friendly too, but wasn't ready to talk about it.

"No problem," he said, looking up from his straw. "What do you say we find a hotel, grab some food, and hit the sack? Then we can be up early in the morning and make it to Seaquarium before lunch." He glanced at her sideways. "There's almost a hundred bucks in the pickle jar. We could go out for a nice dinner if you like. Get dressed up, even."

Violet felt a flutter in her chest. It might have been panic. It might have been the nachos. Or else it was the thought of dressing up and going out with Smitty. Like a date.

Then she thought of her new vow. No matter how lonely she might get, and how cute the blond streaks in Smitty's hair might be, she wasn't jeopardizing her closest remaining friendship to try something that had already failed—spectacularly—once before. She shook her head and ignored the thump of regret. "I don't think that's such a good idea, Smitty. Maybe we should just drive through to Florida tonight."

He grinned crookedly. "Aw, come on, Vi. For old times' sake? I'd like to take you to dinner." He paused. "Although, since we both put about the same amount of money into the jar, I guess I wouldn't really be taking you to dinner, would I? We'd be taking each other, really."

When he put it like that, Violet thought it sounded almost reasonable. And tempting. She wavered until she looked into his eyes and saw shadows of the years that stood between them. She shook her head. "I think I've had about as much 'old times' sake' as I can stand for one day." She gestured around the park. "This was fun, but I think I'm ready to hit the road rather than play another game of 'Remember When?' "

He was quiet a moment, sipping his soda. Then he said, "What *do* you remember, Vi? You said something earlier that's been bothering me. Did you really think I wanted a family more than I wanted you?"

Okaaay. It seemed that he wanted to rehash history after all. Violet had a quick, insane urge to avoid the whole discussion by chucking the nachos in his lap and bolting for the park entrance.

Frankly, the only thing stopping her was the fact that she had nowhere to go but back to Dolphin Friendly, and Smitty was bound to turn up there sooner or later. Besides, there had been times in her life when she would have killed to have had this conversation.

Ten years and one ex-wife ago, she would have given anything to understand why he'd left her the moment he realized that she seriously wanted to wait to get married and have children. Eight years ago when she'd returned to Dolphin Friendly, she would have paid money to understand why he'd barely acknowledged her presence, let alone why he hadn't tried to pick up where they'd left off.

But now? Now it felt like the time for explanations was past. They'd done what they'd done and it was time to live with it and move on.

So she shrugged. "Don't worry about it, Smits. It's ancient history and we got beyond it a long, long time ago."

"Did we?" He leaned forward, his blue eyes intent. She remembered how she used to think those eyes were like the Caribbean, clear and deep at the same time. Now they were just eyes, she told herself. He was just Smitty. "Or is all the arguing we've been doing for the last few years just our way of not having this conversation?"

Violet sat back, stung. "No. I argue with you because you're wrong. There's nothing more sinister about it than that." She sipped her soda and cursed the quiver she felt in her lower lip.

It seemed that Smitty wanted things to change after all. Their pranks and spats energized her. Entertained her. Made her feel like someone on that boat noticed her when Brody and Maddy were so wrapped up in each other that the world seemed to begin and end with them.

"I like fighting with you," she said in a low voice, hating to admit even that much to him.

Smitty leaned back in his chair and smiled crookedly. She saw the little chip on his front tooth where he'd smacked into the wheelhouse one time when *Streaker* was being tossed about by angry seas.

He'd been trying to reach her, Violet remembered, because she'd just rejoined the boat after her sojourn in Puget Sound and was reveling in the heave of the open ocean. She'd insisted on clinging to the forward rail while *Streaker* jolted from wave to wave. Smitty had brought her a life vest and a line he'd tied to one of the docking cleats. If she was going overboard, he'd said, he wanted to have a way to haul her back onto the boat. It wasn't the first time he'd looked after her that way, and it certainly hadn't been the last. Even when their fights were at their most bitter, they'd looked after each other.

And in the end, wasn't that what friends were for?

Smitty saw the look in her eyes change, and wasn't sure whether he should be relieved or terrified. One of the things that had always fascinated him about Violet was her ability to change moods so quickly, so completely that he was left behind in her wake.

He'd once heard an ancient Asian proverb, or maybe it was a curse, he couldn't remember. It said, *May you live in interesting times.* He'd always thought in Violet's case it should've been, *May you love an interesting woman.*

Again, he wasn't sure whether it would be a proverb or a curse. Because he *had* loved Violet. Still did, in an old-flame-turned-best-friend sort of way. And Brody was right. She wasn't happy. Though her eyes now reflected a tolerant sort of fondness, on an overall, day-to-day basis, Violet wasn't happy.

Once, Smitty might have guessed it was because of his marriage to Ellen. But if that were the reason for her unhappiness, she would want to talk about it now, wouldn't she? It was just the two of them. What better time for a conversation that was arguably a decade late? Though he wasn't sure he could excuse all his actions back then, he'd sure like to try. Anything to hear her laugh for real again.

But she didn't want to talk about Ellen. Ergo, her unhappiness came from another source. Brody. And her relationship with Brody was the last thing Smitty wanted to talk about. The subject still made him a little raw. He didn't like to think of his two best friends together. Didn't like to think of her pining for the relationship.

But Violet was special to him, and if she was hurting, then he was too. He could handle this.

So he took a deep breath. Stalled. Choked down a cold nacho. Made a face and said, "It's not that I mind fighting with you, Vi. But Brody's got a point that it's all we do anymore. We used to get along better than this. You started to say something in the river and I interrupted you. So tell me now. What's wrong, are you upset about Brody and Maddy getting married?"

"Brody and Maddy?" She tilted her head, considering, and Smitty began to hope that she wasn't still carrying a torch for the third member of their Musketeer-like group. But his spirits sank again when she said, "I guess that's a big part of it."

He swallowed. Okay. He could do this. He could be the supportive friend if it killed him.

"I know you and he used to be . . . close." He sucked a mouthful of soda and forged on. "But he and Maddy are together now. They love each other."

Violet shrugged and relaxed. "No kidding. That's the prob—" She broke off. Narrowed her eyes at him. "You're not implying that I . . . That Brody and I. . . ." She sat back with a look of part annoyance, part amusement crossing her face. "You are! You think that I'm upset because—Gargk!" Her words were muffled when a stream of water hit her full in the face.

There was a childish giggle from the next table over.

"Violet, what—Glurk!" Smitty turned just in time to catch a mouthful of chlorinated water himself. The next volley flooded the dish with the leftover nachos and splashed Violet's chest.

A small, demonic-looking child at the next table held a mega-soaker in his hands and laughed gleefully as he hosed down their table, their towels, and what was left of their snack.

"Brian Patrick, you stop that this instant!" Rescue appeared in the form of a harried-looking woman with a toddler in tow. The woman grabbed the battery-powered squirt gun from her grinning child and shook her finger. "How many times have I told you not to point this thing at strangers? What did I tell you I was going to do the next time it happened?"

The child toed the ground and stared intently at his feet, but Smitty could see he was far from remorseful.

Violet touched the young mother's arm and gestured at the soaker. The woman grinned and handed Violet the mega-soaker while keeping her tone stern. "Now you apologize to these people right now, and make it good!"

As Smitty watched, little Brian Patrick looked up and said, "I'm very—Eek!" as Violet squirted him.

Back on *Streaker*, they kept the mega-squirt cartridges in the refrigerator so the water was extra cold.

Smitty had been on the receiving end of several sneak attacks in the past, and could only smile and watch as Violet tousled the boy's hair and handed the squirt gun back to the child.

But then an unexpected lump backed up in his throat.

Somewhere along the line, he'd forgotten how good Violet was with kids. How had he forgotten that she loved kids? Maybe, he mused, it had happened the moment she'd rejected the idea of bearing his children and providing him with a family.

Then he registered his own thoughts and stilled. A family. No, that wasn't right. He'd wanted to marry her because he loved her. He'd told her that, a decade ago, in a water park just like this one.

Hadn't he?

"My mom says when I do something wrong, I hafta 'pologize," the kid piped up, not looking very contrite. He grinned from Smitty to Violet. "Sorry, mister. Sorry, lady."

"No problem, kid. Just watch where you point that thing, and listen to your mom, okay? She seems like a wise lady." Violet waved to him and then turned back to Smitty. "You about ready to go?"

But the boy's words rattled in his head. *When I do something wrong, I have to apologize.*

He was beginning to think he'd done something

very, very wrong ten years earlier. He took her hand. "I'm sorry, Vi. I never meant to hurt you back then. I hope you'll believe it. I truly am sorry."

She sobered instantly, caught her breath, and seemed to lean towards him. The intimacy of their earlier conversation dropped around them like a cloak of emotion. "Sorry for what exactly?"

He cast back through the years for the day that it had all gone wrong for them. The day that had spelled the end of their grad school romance. The day at the water park when he'd asked her to marry him and she'd turned him down. He said, "I'm sorry I made you think that I wanted a family more than I wanted you."

Her mouth twisted in a frown and she drew back. "Don't apologize for what I thought, Smitty. Apologize for what you did. I loved you and you didn't wait for me." She pulled her hand away. "I needed you like I needed my next breath back then. Foolish of me, wasn't it?"

She turned away and gathered their trash with restless hands. He had to stop himself from grabbing her and shaking her until her teeth rattled. It made no sense. "Then why did you turn me down? I wanted to *marry* you, for heaven's sake."

"You wanted to get married. There's a difference." She pitched their garbage into a barrel and draped her towel over her shoulders.

"What does that mean?" he snapped, feeling irritation and confusion jumble together in his stomach. "I loved you. I wanted to marry you, have a family with you. Why is that so wrong?"

She spun on him, and Smitty was surprised to see a suspicious glimmer in her eyes.

It must be a trick of the light. Violet never cried. He was sure of it.

Jabbing a finger into his chest, she said, "If you were so all-fired in love with me, then why'd you turn around and marry Ellen not a month later?" Her voice cracked.

"Ellen?" he practically bellowed, then lowered his voice when he realized they were attracting attention in the water park café. He hissed, "What does this have to do with Ellen? I didn't start seeing her until after we broke up. How is this her fault?"

"It's *not* her fault, and we didn't break up." Violet grabbed her towel and reached down to unfasten the locker key from its ankle strap. "You left me."

"Because you didn't want to marry me," he countered, feeling utterly lost. What was he missing here?

"I never said I didn't want to marry you." She had her back to him now, and her words were muffled.

Smitty shook his head in bafflement. "Sure you did. Well, first you gave me that line about only having been away from home for a few months, and having our whole lives in front of us, and how we should wait until after we graduated . . ." He trailed off, because suddenly it didn't sound like as much of a pile of tuna as it had when he was twenty-something and a confused mess of hormones and loneliness.

"It wasn't a line, idiot." Her voice cracked again and she still wouldn't face him. "It was the truth."

He tried to dredge up some of the anger he'd carried towards her for so long. "But if you wanted to marry me eventually, what difference would a few months or years have made?"

He could see the top of her head nod. "Exactly. What difference would a little time have made? Not one bit, if you'd wanted me. But you'd just lost your mother. You were alone in the world and you wanted to put down roots. You wanted an instant family and I wasn't ready to be that for you."

Violet had obviously thought this through just as much as he had. Too bad they'd come to opposite conclusions.

"If you'd loved me, then you would've believed that a few months either way wouldn't matter. You would've married me," he said. He'd told himself the words so many times they even sounded true now.

She shook her head and there were tears in her eyes, he was sure of it now. "If you'd loved me, you would've waited until I was ready to marry you. But you didn't." She sniffed. "You married an organic pig farmer named Ellen instead."

He put a hand on her back. Her shoulders shook. "Violet. . . ."

She sniffed, and he broke. "Aw, Vi. I'm so sorry." He gathered her into his arms, not sure whether she'd cry or punch him. This new, emotional Violet was a stranger to him.

She held herself stiff for a moment, then sagged against him. Her arms crept around his waist and she sighed. "God, Smits. We should've had this conversation years ago. Does it sound as stupid to you as it does to me now? Quibbling over months when it's obvious neither of us wanted to get married to the other? You're right. If we had, the timing wouldn't have mattered one way or the other."

Though he wasn't sure he agreed—he'd wanted to marry her, darn it—Smitty dropped his cheek to her hair and held her.

He'd forgotten how good it felt. How perfectly they fit together. "I'm sorry," he murmured. "I didn't do it right."

She sniffed once and pushed away from him, leaving the air to cool his chest and cheek where contact had warmed them. "Neither of us did it right. We were young and stupid, and more in love with the idea of being in love than we were with one another. And now we've spent most of a decade being angry with each other for acting like kids. Well guess what? We *were* kids. But we're grown-ups now, even if we don't always act like it." She stuck out a hand. "Can we call a truce? Make friends? It's what we're here for, right?"

Smitty stared at the hand for a moment, mistrusting that ten years could be wiped away that easily. Not sure he wanted it to be. Something important had just passed between them, but he wasn't yet sure what it was.

"Come on, let's shake on it." She waved her hand and her perfectly painted nails flashed. "Then let's get on the road. We can make it to the Seaquarium by morning."

He took her hand and held it rather than shaking it. "No fancy dinner for us tonight then? Not even to celebrate our new level of understanding and the end of our feuding days?"

She avoided his gaze. "I don't think so." But she sounded sad. Almost wistful. She slid her eyes to his, then away. "I've always valued our friendship, Smits, even when we've mostly been fighting. I don't want to endanger it by turning it into something . . . else, okay? We tried that once and it didn't work. I value you too much to try again. I think we should just be . . . friends, and leave it at that, okay?"

Tugging her hand away, she wrapped her towel around her waist as though suddenly self-conscious about the amount of skin her bikini revealed. She turned and headed for the locker area, calling over her shoulder, "I'll meet you by the front entrance in five. And I'm really glad we got all that sorted out."

She disappeared into the ladies' changing area, leaving Smitty standing near the nacho stand, shaking his head. His body was warm where it had touched hers. His hand tingled faintly, and he had the insane urge to chase after her and play this whole scene over again, differently.

Because as far as he was concerned, their conversation had raised as many questions as it had answered. And he'd be darned if he let her finish this road trip without answering a few more of them.

Like whether her blood heated when they were together. Or whether her heart pounded when they touched.

Whether she ever wished things had been different. And whether she had the guts to try again.

Chapter Six

The refrigerator truck's engine hummed a steady monotone as they crossed the border into Florida late that night. Violet glanced over at her passenger and was relieved to see that Smitty had finally dropped off to sleep.

When they'd gotten back on the road, he'd tried to talk about what had happened at the water park, but she hadn't been ready. So they'd driven in silence for a time, with the questions humming between them, unasked.

Was it really so simple? Had she spent the last ten years blaming him completely for something that had been both their faults—or really nobody's fault at all?

She shook her head and changed lanes. Perhaps it was that simple. But it really wasn't simple at all, because during the course of their day at the water park, she'd realized she was in deeper trouble than she'd thought.

Every time Smitty had glanced at her, it felt like a caress. Every time he touched her—to help her onto a ride, or to draw her attention to a pretty scene—she felt like liquid fire had been poured through her veins.

Before, she'd blamed it on irritation. On *Streaker's* close quarters and the inevitable awareness that developed when two people worked together as much as they did. Now she acknowledged she was attracted to him. And that was a bad thing. There was no room on *Streaker* for another couple, and there was sure as heck no room for a breakup.

It had been weird enough when she and Brody dissolved their so-called relationship, when frankly there hadn't been much regret on either side. But she knew from experience that breaking up with Smitty brought forth very different emotions.

Wrenching, tearing emotions she'd rather not relive.

Ten years ago, she'd run away—straight to that research project on Puget Sound. But where could she go this time? Dolphin Friendly was her family, and they couldn't afford to have her gone just as the new stranding center was going on-line. Or could they?

No, she decided. She couldn't leave. And if she and Smitty started something again and it failed, she wouldn't be able to stay.

The man in question stirred in his sleep and muttered something. She glanced over and was rewarded by the play of streetlight over his familiar features. He was going to have a heck of a sore neck if he kept sleeping like that—all jammed between the uncomfortable edge of the bench seat and the smeared window. Violet debated moving him, but decided to leave well enough alone. She didn't want him to wake up now. In the dead of the night, cocooned in the cab of the humming truck, it would be too easy to say something she'd regret during the day.

He stirred again and mumbled, "Violet? Vi?" The words were thick with sleep and precious because of it. She dreamed of him sometimes and woke up feeling warm and loved. Other times, she woke feeling lonely. Maybe now he was dreaming of her.

She drove with one hand, reached over and touched his clenched fist with the other. "I'm here

Smits. It's going to be okay. We'll find a way to get along so we can both stay with Dolphin Friendly. That's all that matters."

Mumbling something else, he opened his hand and tangled his fingers with hers, the way he used to when they were together, and she felt a dull ache under her breastbone.

Violet slid her hand free as the truck labored up a gentle Florida hill. She stomped on the clutch and muttered, "We've both got to stay with the group. Nothing else matters."

Then she changed gears.

Smitty woke up just as they eased into the back lot of the Seaquarium. From the looks of the sky, it was early morning. He wasn't sure what day it was, but he was convinced that he'd never been quite as sticky and sore as he was at that moment. In his opinion, which he'd shared with Violet when they'd stopped to brush their teeth with iron-tainted truck stop water, not even a four-day stranding rescue in a sludge-filled inlet could compare to the experience of riding in a non-air-conditioned refrigerator truck all the way from Cape Cod to Florida.

Violet was still driving, as she had been since the night before. She'd snarled when he'd offered to switch, so he'd given up and gone back to sleep.

She'd apparently opted to head straight for the Sea-quarium rather than stopping off at a motel to shower and change.

He glanced over at the driver's seat. Her brunette hair was long and lustrous, caught up in a casual ponytail that made her look about eighteen. Her nails were perfect, her khaki shorts neatly pressed, and the floaty blouse she'd tied over another of those cling-ing tank tops added just the right touch of girl.

Of course she hadn't wanted to stop and refresh herself. She was born refreshed.

He lifted himself off the passenger side window that had formed his pillow since Georgia, and tried to sit up straight like his mother had always badgered him to do when he was a boy. Every muscle in his body protested the action with howls of pain. He scrubbed a hand through his hair and wondered whether it was possible that he'd actually made his teeth dirtier by brushing them at that truck stop.

"We're here," Violet sang, sounding annoyingly happy. "And look, there's a welcoming committee."

Sure enough, there was a small group clustered around the back gate that led into the stranding res-cue staging area of the Seaquarium. Smitty and Vi-olet both knew their way around the place, since Dolphin Friendly had worked out of the Seaquarium several years ago, compiling stranding data for the Florida coast.

Because of the familiarity, Smitty was annoyed that he felt like such a mess when they arrived. These people are researchers, he assured himself, they understand that being rumpled-looking is part of the job . . . even if your traveling companion looks like she just stepped off the cover of a fashion magazine.

He and Violet swung out of the cab to a chorus of hellos and welcomes, and Smitty tried not to notice that all of the Seaquarium staff members were dressed in perfectly pressed khaki shorts and logo polo shirts.

"Violet! Smitty!" A tall man stepped ahead of the others and spread his arms in welcome. He looked familiar in a slick, well-groomed sort of way. His dark hair was disheveled and probably trained to stay that way for the duration of the day. His teeth were perfectly white, his tan perfectly even, and the legs that stuck out of his perfectly pressed shorts were . . . well, perfect.

Smitty couldn't place him immediately—he hadn't been one of the staff members they'd dealt with at the Seaquarium before—but he was pretty sure the guy was going to irritate him, which was surprising, as Smitty wasn't one for snap judgments and he liked just about everyone. Except this guy.

That thought became a certainty when Violet whooped and jumped into the other man's arms.

"Chaz! What are you doing here?" She hugged him and Smitty ground his teeth.

He was right. Now that he knew who Mr. Perfect was, Smitty knew for sure that he didn't like the guy much. Chaz Trowt—with a name like that, he should've gone into fisheries biology, not marine mammology—had been a year or two ahead of them at U.C. Santa Cruz. He'd been a straight-A student, president of half the clubs on campus, and had always had a pack of women on his heels.

Finished with his excessive welcome of Violet, Chaz turned and held out his hand. "And Smitty! I haven't seen you in ages. You look . . ." he glanced up and down Smitty's rumpled, travel-weary form and finished with a lame, "good."

Smitty shook his hand because he couldn't think of a graceful way not to. "Chaz. I didn't know you worked here." He glanced between Violet and Chaz and narrowed his eyes when he noticed how close they were standing. "And I didn't know you two were so *friendly*."

Chaz looked surprised by Smitty's scowl. He took a step back towards his coworkers. "Violet and I worked together on the Puget Sound project. We got to know each other pretty well, but fell out of contact after. You know how it is." His eyes darted back and forth between Smitty and Violet and one eyebrow lifted in silent question. "I didn't know you two were back together. Brody didn't mention it when he called to say you were on your way."

Violet shook her head in quick denial. "Oh no, we're not together, Chaz. We're just friends, right, Smitty?"

He felt her elbow in his ribs and nodded, irritated with himself that he was annoyed. That's what they'd decided on at the water park, wasn't it? Friends. They'd called a truce and agreed to leave their past behind. So why did the idea of her snuggling up to Chaz-the-Perfect irritate him so much?

"Oh good! Then I'd love to take you out to dinner tonight, Vi. For old times' sake." Chaz smiled dazzlingly and Smitty wondered whether he had ever tried to jump off the side of a research vessel with his swim fins glued to the deck.

"Sorry," Smitty said without a trace of remorse. "We've already made plans for dinner tonight."

Violet looked up at him in surprise. "We have?"

"Of course. Remember? We have to spend the specimen jar money." They'd added to it the night before when he'd wanted to stop and buy Georgia peaches and she hadn't, and again when she'd needed a bathroom break a half hour after they'd stopped for gas. They were up to almost a hundred and fifty dollars now. "There won't be time to do it on the way home, and by the time we get back to Smugglers Cove things will be in an uproar, getting ready for the big opening."

She nodded and Chaz looked handsomely crestfallen. Then Violet snapped her fingers. "Chaz! Why don't you come to dinner with us? We can all catch up on old times, and there's more than enough money in the fight jar to pay for all of us. Please say you'll come!"

Smitty couldn't very well argue with her logic—except that he'd wanted Violet all to himself for one dinner. Just to test their new truce, of course, not like it was a real date or anything. But it seemed that she was bound and determined to spend her evening with Perfect Chaz.

It was funny. He didn't remember having disliked Chaz this much when they'd all been in school together.

Clearly sensing a dangerous undercurrent, Chaz glanced from one to the other. "Are you sure?"

"Of course," Violet answered for both of them. "We'd love to have you along. Meet us in the Seaquarium Hotel lobby after the park closes—say seven—and we'll go from there, okay? And if you don't mind driving, that'd be great. Our wheels are less than stylish."

Chaz nodded, Smitty grumbled, and the welcoming committee—some of whom had started shifting restlessly during this exchange—ushered the newcomers into the Seaquarium to meet their new passenger.

Jasper the sea lion was huge and very, very friendly.

Violet discovered this when she leaned down to examine his feeding chart and he poked his whiskered nose through the mesh of his holding pen and gave her a wet, fishy kiss on the cheek. "Ugh! Um . . . I mean, thanks, Jasper."

Smitty snickered and she glared at him. He'd been easier to deal with when he'd been fast asleep in the truck. Then at least she could glance at him from time to time and indulge in bittersweet memories of the good times they'd had together. Now that he was awake—and looking as devastatingly rumpled and unshaven as she'd ever seen him—he was bothering her again on a very deep, very primitive level.

She'd thought that once they talked about their grad school breakup and put it in the past, her characteristic twitchiness around him would be gone. She'd always blamed it on leftover anger from the way he'd married Ellen right after she'd turned him down. But if anything, it seemed worse. She was aware of his every motion. His every mood.

That's why she'd been so glad to see Chaz. Like Brody, he could provide a badly needed buffer.

"Hork! Hork!" Jasper applauded himself for the kiss and Violet grabbed a corner of Smitty's shirt and used it to wipe her face off.

"Hey!"

She shrugged. "Like anyone will notice another smear on your ensemble."

She had a fleeting thought that maybe she'd borrowed his shirt to warn the circling vultures away. The women who worked at the Seaquarium were already giving Smitty the once-over . . . and his filthy shirt was the last thing they were looking at. Violet bared her teeth at a particularly interested-looking blond whose logo polo shirt was a wee bit tight.

"That's Candi with an 'i'," Chaz murmured in her ear, noticing the direction of Violet's gaze. Then he raised his voice. "And I've got a great idea. Candi, why don't you join us for dinner tonight as well? You can be Smitty's guest and I'll be Violet's. Four is a much more comfortable number than three, don't you think?"

Violet winced at the idea, but her protest was drowned out by Candi's squeal of glee. Smitty just glowered, which seemed to be his fallback expression of the morning, and the arrangements were made.

"Can we *please*," Violet said through clenched teeth, "get on with this? We're going to load Jasper first thing tomorrow morning and drive him round the clock until we get him to Smugglers Cove right before the opening ceremonies. That's the way Brody has it planned. So we're going to need to know how to work the commands you've taught him for the ceremony. Chaz, I'd like you to run us through his routine, please."

"Of course, Vi." One of the other women produced an enormous pair of fake scissors, a dog whistle, and a bucket of fish. Chaz hopped into Jasper's holding pen and gave three short peeps on the whistle, which brought the enormous creature out of the water and up onto a floating dock.

At sixteen years old, Jasper was a full-grown California sea lion, and looked much like the wild ones off the Monterey coast. She might have been saddened that the twelve-hundred-pound animal lived in captivity, even though his accommodations were large and well designed, but she could also see the gnarled white scar running down his flank, and could tell that one of his hind flippers—which sea lions use for steering—was damaged.

The Seaquarium was primarily a stranding rescue center. Its seal, dolphin, and manatee educational programs were populated with animals that had been rescued and were too badly hurt for rehabilitation. Its sea lion show was made up of animals who'd been rescued from their native waters off California and shipped to Florida for placement.

She watched Chaz run Jasper through a warm-up routine of spins, jumps, and ball balancing, and she felt herself relax. The sea lion was obviously enjoying his work. As the behaviors grew more complex, Chaz provided a running commentary on the cognitive research that was also taking place at the Seaquarium, using the sea lions and a few rescued dolphins. Violet soon found herself nodding and asking questions.

It wasn't quite the open seas that she loved, but she decided it wasn't bad either. The research done at the Seaquarium provided information that would help Dolphin Friendly with its new stranding research center.

"It's all based on targeting, see?" Chaz demonstrated by cueing Jasper to place his nose on a ball. Wherever he moved the ball, Jasper's nose followed. "Just say 'Jasper, target' and he'll latch on to the prop." He demonstrated with the fake scissors and Violet saw Smitty nod.

He didn't seem to be frowning as hard as he had been. Maybe he was looking forward to dinner with Candi.

Now Violet scowled.

"Why don't you two come in here and practice with him?" Chaz handed over the props and ushered her and Smitty into the pen. "Just do what I showed you, and if he gives you a behavior that's even close to what you want, reward him with a short blast on the whistle and a piece of fish. Once he's got the idea, you can shape the behavior until it's where you want it. That's called 'modeling,' or 'shaping.' "

Smitty took the trainer's place, and Violet felt incredibly foolish holding a piece of ribbon and an oversized pair of fake scissors. They ran through the behavior a few times until Jasper was taking the scissors in his mouth and using them to 'cut' the ribbon on Smitty's command.

"Okay, now switch so he's heard the cues from both of you," Chaz suggested. "That way you'll be all ready for Brody's show the day after tomorrow."

Violet was happy to relinquish the ribbon, but with her, Smitty, and Jasper all on the float at once, it was difficult to swap places. She tried to edge around Jasper's rear end so she wouldn't have to go near Smitty, but a couple of low, annoyed-sounding grunts from the sea lion let her know that wasn't going to work.

She reversed direction and tried to slide past Smitty without touching him as he tried to do the same, but her foot slipped on a fallen piece of fish. She squeaked as she fell towards the water, grabbing for Smitty, who tried to catch her. He snagged a handful of her shirt . . . and they both pitched into the water of the sea lion's tank.

Chapter Seven

"Hork, hork, hork!" Jasper barked joyfully and hopped into the water, swimming around his two new best friends as Smitty clawed his way back to the surface and hauled Violet up with him.

Somehow they'd wound up tangled together on the way down and her arms were still wrapped around his waist. He glanced over at the dock and saw about a hundred amused-looking faces—well, at least twenty—peering down at them.

"HORK!" Jasper swam right up and bayed in Smitty's ear, making his head ring with sea lion enthusiasm.

"You guys want a hand, or are you enjoying it in

there?" came Chaz's voice, and Violet must have realized that she was snuggled up against her least favorite person, because she pushed herself away from
Smitty with such force that he went under again.

When he bobbed back up, he tried to be a gentle-
man and help her up onto the float, but when he
grabbed her ankle to boost her up, his hand slipped
on her wet leg and he accidentally grabbed her khaki-
clad rump.

Violet squeaked and seemed to leap up the rest of
the way onto the float. "Well, I never—"

Smitty was pretty sure she *had*, on at least a few
other occasions, but he didn't think now was a good
time to mention it. Instead he said, "Now Violet, I
didn't mean—"

"We had an agreement!" she yelled, "A truce!"
And she dumped the bucket of fish on his head.

"Hork!" The sea lion's delighted bark drowned out
Smitty's less-than-delighted response, and Jasper
darted around collecting bits of mackerel as Violet
stomped squishily out of the pen.

There was a moment of stunned, amused silence.

Chaz finally stepped forward and offered Smitty a
hand. There was a barely masked chuckle in his
voice when he asked, "Want me to help you out of
there, or do you like Jasper licking fish out of your
hair?"

Smitty grumbled under his breath and let Chaz haul him out of the tank. Once he was on the dock and a rapidly spreading puddle was forming at his feet, he shrugged and forced a chuckle. "Well, when we got here I was wishing for a shower. Guess I got my wish."

Chaz sniffed and wrinkled his perfect nose. "If you say so. But if I were you, I'd still vote for the shower—at least before we all go to dinner." He paused and cleared his throat. "Are you sure there's nothing going on with you and Violet? I don't want to get in the middle of it if there is."

Smitty shook his head, discouraged. Little droplets of water sprinkled from his hair. "There's nothing going on with us. Right now, I'm pretty sure she hates me or something."

"Or something," Chaz repeated.

Smitty rolled his eyes to the ceiling. "Why does everyone keep saying that? What do you know that I don't about my own life?"

"I don't know anything about your life," Chaz allowed, "but I remember Violet when she first joined the Puget Sound study. She was pretty broken up about you marrying that Ellen girl from the agronomy program."

"I know what program Ellen was in. She was my wife." He never quite understood how he'd come to be married to a woman who'd majored in organic pig farming. He'd woken up one day about a year after his mother's death and found that Violet was gone, he was married to a woman who didn't love the ocean, and there was a gaping hole in his chest where his heart had been.

Somewhere in the twelve months following the death of his last remaining family member, he'd made some very bad decisions.

Chaz nodded. "Of course. Regardless, Violet did almost nothing other than work for the first year she was on the Puget project. She volunteered for all the extra shifts, did the sonar logs when she wasn't on call, and slept most of the rest of the time." He paused, then lowered the boom. "And she cried."

Smitty almost scoffed at the absurdity of it. "Violet never cries." Though she had sniffled against his chest the day before. But that didn't quite count as tears.

Chaz shrugged. "Believe what you will, but take it from me, she was a mess. She got over you— eventually—and decided to go back to Dolphin Friendly. I've seen her one other time since, when you guys were working off Chincoteague Island and the group I was with passed through, and she seemed happy enough. But she doesn't seem so happy now."

Not knowing what to say, Smitty nodded reluctantly and thought of her failed relationship with Brody. "I know. I wish I could fix it, but I don't think it has anything to do with me this time."

Chaz shrugged. "Suit yourself. And don't say I didn't ask. I believe in playing fair, and you just declared the field open for a kickoff." He sniffed, grinned, and said, "Not to be rude or anything, Smitty, but I'd suggest you hike across the street to the hotel and hit the showers before the play commences."

Showered and refreshed, Violet sought out the manatees. Oh, how she loved manatees. She'd been fascinated with them ever since the first time she'd seen a picture of one in the encyclopedia at her Midwest grade school. Meeting them in person had only strengthened the emotion.

They were like giant, animated sofas.

Although it seemed a little disloyal of her—being a member of Dolphin Friendly and all—she loved manatees more than anything, though she'd never been able to work with them full-time. Now, she grinned in anticipation as she sat at the edge of the wide, shallow tank and dipped her feet in the brackish water. A trio of the young animals swam slowly towards her at top speed, which meant they took almost a minute to reach her.

There were lettuce leaves and other tasty offerings floating about the tank, so the strange, soft-looking creatures weren't looking to her for a handout. They simply wanted to cuddle. When one of them reached her, it began to suck on her toes, and she felt the rasp of the dull bony ridges that they used to chew their plant meals. They had no teeth. Everything about them was soft and slow.

Harmless. Vulnerable.

Violet rubbed the baby manatee's broad, flat back with her other foot and winced at the slashing white scars. "You've got to be smarter about avoiding those motor boats, little guy," she said to the brownish gray creature.

The size of a full-grown seal now, the manatee would grow to a thousand pounds or more and would rarely swim faster than seven or eight miles an hour. When it was returned to the brackish rivers of southern Florida—this one was lucky and would heal enough to be released—its poor eyesight and lousy hearing would combine to make it an accident waiting to happen for unwary motor boaters.

There weren't many left in their native Florida waters.

"Hopefully they'll find you a river that's off-limits to boats, huh?" she said, and rubbed the broad forehead with her hand. The manatee's walrus-like whiskers tickled her palm, and the other two rescued babies gently crowded her legs, vying for attention in slow motion.

"We'll do our best."

Violet started, having not heard anyone come up behind her. Then she relaxed, recognizing Chaz's voice. He joined her on the edge of the manatee pool and dipped his legs into the water beside hers.

She sighed and kept rubbing the manatees with her feet. One rolled over so she could reach its tummy. At least that's what she thought it intended. The maneuver took so long she couldn't quite tell, and their backs and bellies looked pretty much the same. "Sorry about dumping the bucket of fish in Jasper's pool. I hope it didn't mess up his feedings for the day."

She wasn't sure what had come over her—and she was heartily embarrassed by the scene. It was one thing for her and Smitty to squabble in front of Brody and the interns. It was quite another for them to act unprofessional in front of colleagues. But Smitty's touch had startled her beyond words. Her reaction had stemmed as much from the sudden blast of heat that had followed his accidental grope as it had from real offense.

Frankly, she'd snarled at Smitty because she'd liked him touching her—and that was just what she was trying to avoid. They could be friends, but not more.

The *more* was just too risky.

Chaz shrugged as though it didn't matter. "No problem. It livened up our morning and Jasper is fine. We were planning on keeping him a little hungry this evening anyway because you're transporting him tomorrow. A big breakfast today is the least of his worries."

Violet glanced over at his profile and remembered when all the girls—and after the pain of Smitty's marriage had dulled some, herself included—had drooled over him during their Puget Sound days, just as the grad students had chased both him and Brody at U.C. Santa Cruz. Now Chaz was just Chaz, like Brody was just Brody.

They were safe.

She smiled as the first manatee slowly pushed the other two away so he could have her feet all to himself. "It's good to see you, Chaz. And I'm glad you're involved with Seaquarium. It's an excellent group."

"We've just gotten funding for two research boats and a team. I'm hiring now," he said conversationally, but the tone in his voice had Violet sitting up. He continued, "We'll run one boat part-time out to open ocean to bring some of our in-house research out into real life."

She couldn't stop herself from asking, "And the rest of the time?"

Chaz quirked a smile. "Inland work. We'll send a team into the estuaries, the mangroves, and the brackish rivers to see what we can do to help these guys." He scratched one of the baby manatees above its tiny eye with his big toe. "Because God knows, they need all the help they can get. Every year their population drops lower. They need someone on their side, Violet. You know that."

Violet nodded, heart racing. Then she blurted out, "Are you saying what I think you're saying?"

"Well, I'm not looking to poach one of Brody's best people." Chaz paused to let her know that's exactly what he wanted to do. "But I'm interviewing team leaders right now."

He glanced as his dive watch and faked surprise. "Will you look at the time? I've got to finish up for the day before we head out for dinner." He gave her arm a friendly squeeze. "See you later."

When he was gone, leaving her alone with the manatees and her own thoughts, Violet slid into the water, not caring that her tank top and shorts wouldn't think much of the plan. Not caring that lettuce leaves were tangling in her hair and sticking to her legs. She floated on her back, closed her eyes, and felt the bump of soft gray-brown noses and the slide of rubbery hide as the manatees welcomed her to their home.

She felt Smitty's nearness before she heard his approach, a sort of preternatural awareness she'd lately labeled irritation, but had once called love.

"Thought I'd find you here," he said by way of announcing his presence. "I remember you spent a lot of time with the manatees when Dolphin Friendly worked at Seaquarium before. You've always loved these guys."

She opened her eyes and saw him standing at the edge of the pool, leaning casually against an upright. He'd showered and changed, though he hadn't shaved. The reddish stubble glowed against his tan and her fingers itched to touch it.

"Forgot my razor," he said, reading her mind like he used to do.

"Sorry about the fish," she said.

He nodded. "Sorry about the butt grab. It was an accident."

They were silent for a moment, then she said, "Chaz offered me a team down here. Ocean part-time, manatees part-time." She wasn't sure what kind of a reaction she was looking for from Smitty. Part of her wanted him to drop to his knees and beg her not to leave Dolphin Friendly. Part of her wanted him to tell her it was a good career move and that she should take it.

Either way, she was disappointed when he merely raised an eyebrow and asked, "You gonna take it?"

She swam over to the side and hoisted herself out of the manatee pool, shedding lettuce and carrots as she emerged from the friendly water. Once she was sitting on the side, she shrugged and said, "I don't know. It's tempting, but . . . I don't know."

Smitty didn't say a thing, just kept staring down into the manatee's pool. But his fists were clenched.

Irritated, though not sure what she wanted from him, Violet got to her feet, dripping. "Well, I've ruined that shower. I'm going to head back to the hotel and get ready for dinner. See you in the lobby about seven?"

He nodded and clenched his jaw. She waited for a moment to see if she was going to get a better response than that. When she didn't, she shook her head and squished in the direction of the hotel.

She didn't turn around when he called her name.

But when she heard the sloppy thump of a head of wet lettuce hitting the wall behind her, she smiled and the tight band around her heart loosened a bit.

He cared. He just didn't know what to do about it any more than she did.

Chapter Eight

Promptly at seven that evening, Violet stepped out of the hotel elevators and Smitty felt the air back up in his lungs. She was wearing a soft purple shirt and a narrow black skirt that was slit high on her leg. Her hair was perfect—as always—and he'd bet she'd painted her nails to match the blouse.

He grinned as she joined the little party in the lobby and a quick glance confirmed that not only were her nails painted a glowing purple, they were decorated with little winking stones.

"You look simply stunning, Violet." Smitty glared at Chaz when the slick devil followed up his compliment by kissing Violet on the cheek and offering her his arm. "Shall we?"

"I was going to say that too," Smitty blurted out. "That you look nice and all." He suddenly felt about twelve years old.

Violet lifted an eyebrow. "Really?" She shrugged and the purple blouse shimmered in the light of the hotel chandelier. "Well, better late than never, I suppose."

And though that probably should have annoyed him, Smitty found himself grinning at the bite in her tone. Ever since they'd left Farewell it felt like they'd been circling around each other awkwardly. Finally she sounded like the Violet he knew and . . . well, the Violet he knew.

Which is why it irked him to see her walk out of the hotel on Chaz's arm.

"Ready?"

Startled by the woman's voice, Smitty looked down. He'd forgotten Candi had come along as his "date," thanks to Chaz the Magnificent. Smitty forced a grin and offered his arm. "Of course."

He didn't have anything against Candi—she seemed like a perfectly lovely woman with perfectly large—er, lovely features. And she worked at Seaquarium, so by definition she escaped the "I don't date non-marine biologists" vow he'd made the day Ellen left him to marry a fellow farmer. But he was in a sour mood—had been ever since Violet had announced that she was thinking of leaving Dolphin Friendly to work down here with the manatees. With Chaz.

Smitty's jaw started to ache and he realized he was grinding his teeth. Again. If he didn't watch it, he'd be down to nubs by the time they got home to Smugglers Cove.

Chaz drove to the restaurant with Violet beside him, leaving Smitty and Candi to squeeze together in the sports car's tiny backseat. By the time they parked at the little fish place that Chaz insisted Violet "would just love," Smitty was pretty sure he'd be having nightmares for a week that would revolve around Candi's cloying chocolate-scented perfume and a big-busted blond octopus.

He scrambled out of the car and sucked in a big lungful of clean, non-chocolaty air. Then he noticed that Chaz had gallantly opened Violet's door for her and was assisting her out of the low-slung car. Ashamed, Smitty turned back and helped Candi, who had somehow managed to get herself tangled in her seat belt.

His mother had raised him right, Smitty thought, even if he forgot about it now and then.

Resigned to the fact that Violet was enjoying the other man's attention, Smitty escorted his own date into the restaurant and tried not to think that it was going to be a very long night.

Candi's annoying giggle rose above the sedate rumble of the other diners' voices and Violet tried not to glare when she looked over and saw Smitty lean down to murmur something to the ultra-perky blond. He was rewarded with another giggle and his square, white teeth flashed when he nodded.

"Isn't that right, Violet?" Chaz's question startled her, and she tried to remember what they'd been talking about. She sipped her soda and bought some time by snagging another pink shrimp from the huge appetizer they'd ordered.

Luckily, Chaz answered for her, which would have been irritating if she'd actually been paying attention. "Of course it's right." And he went on with an enthusiastic description of the new online manatee population flowcharts he'd been creating.

The Seaquarium, in conjunction with other local agencies, had developed a network of observers who recorded manatee sightings in the rivers and estuaries near their homes. Many of the animals were tagged, and the colors and numbers of their tags helped identify them for the database, which tracked the animals' movement over time.

Violet nodded and tried to ignore the fact that Candi had just fed Smitty a shrimp. What was the problem? Why couldn't she keep her mind on what Chaz was saying? Normally, manatee conversation would've had her fully involved and excited with the prospect of helping the soft, slow-moving creatures. But tonight she could barely concentrate as Chaz described the work he hoped to accomplish with his new team.

All she was thinking about was reaching across the table and yanking on a big handful of bottle-bleach blond hair until the other woman squealed for mercy.

She was, Violet realized, completely and miserably jealous. The sight of Smitty enjoying himself with another woman—a shorter, sweeter, younger, blonder woman—was making her crazy. Because if he was showing interest in Candi, that meant he'd realized the same thing she had following Brody's marriage—that it was time for the three original members of Dolphin Friendly to think about growing up, settling down, and pushing the organization in new directions.

Miles away, she'd taken a moment to look back on the last few months and acknowledge that that realization was part of why she'd played trick after trick on him in the months following their friends' marriage. If she could keep Smitty acting young, acting silly like he always had, then she could keep things the way they'd always been.

Because if Smitty grew up and settled down, where would that leave her?

Alone. Lonely. The odd man out.

"Vi? You okay?" She glanced up to find Smitty looking at her with concern written on his dear, handsome face.

She smiled and nodded, hoping he wouldn't pick that moment to read her mind. "Sure. Fine."

How would it feel if she didn't see him every day? She glanced at Chaz, who'd engaged Candi in a spot of in-house gossip about one of the vet techs, who was apparently having a red-hot affair with the balding forty-something head administrator. She could work with these people. It wouldn't be hard to fit in.

Glancing down at the table to where Candi's chipped pink nails rested lightly on Smitty's forearm, Violet grimaced. It would be easier not to see him at all than it would be to see him fall in love with another woman. Again.

So, very deliberately, Violet touched Chaz's hand and regained his attention. She gave him her best smile and said, "So tell me more about your plans for the new team."

He'd been right. It had been an endlessly long night, Smitty thought, as he slumped in the corner of the elevator, blissfully alone. After Chaz and Violet had elected to stay at the restaurant and listen to the live jazz quartet—and Smitty knew for a fact that Violet wasn't partial to horns—he and Candi had taken a cab back to the hotel.

He hadn't been able to think of a good reason to refuse her invitation to share a last drink at the bar, but an hour later he was wishing passionately that he'd managed to find a reason. Any reason. Because his head was killing him, and he was pretty sure that the next time she giggled, he was going postal.

Then lady luck had smiled on him in the form of two Seaquarium employees who'd waved to Candi and asked her to join them.

They must've seen the desperation in her date's eyes, Smitty thought as he dragged himself down the hall towards his room, fumbling for the key card. He wanted nothing more than to sleep through the night so it would be morning and he and Violet could load up their passenger and head for Smugglers Cove. Because if they stayed here another day, Smitty was sure he would go crazy and do something he'd regret for the rest of his life.

Like get down on his knees and beg Violet not to leave Dolphin Friendly.

He glared at the door to her room—next to his— as he swiped the key card for the third time. The darned things never worked right for him. Ever. He would've banged on her door to see if she'd let him in through the locked door that connected their rooms, but why bother? She wasn't back yet. She was still out with Chaz.

He swiped the card again. Cursed. He drew back his foot to kick the door.

"Here, let me." Violet deftly slipped the key card from his suddenly nerveless fingers, swiped it through the lock, and pushed open the door when the light flickered green and the mechanism clicked open. "You never did figure key cards out, did you?"

Smitty didn't answer. He was too busy gaping. She was holding a bucket full of ice packed around a can of soda. Her feet were bare. Her hair was down around her shoulders like he rarely ever saw it—she almost always wore it up for convenience. And she was wearing an oversized T-shirt covered with pictures of big, mean sharks surrounding a single worried-looking goldfish.

Still holding his door open, she cocked her head. "You okay, Smits?"

He felt an odd stirring in his chest. Possibly the extra spicy calamari.

Or else it was *something else*.

"Don't go," he blurted out.

She raised an eyebrow. "Where? To my room? In

case you hadn't noticed, it's almost midnight. You and . . . Candi must've lost track of time."

Which made him wonder how long she'd been back at the hotel. She and Chaz the Magnificent must not have stayed at the restaurant long. He smiled at the thought, but felt his nerves sizzle when he said, "No, don't leave Dolphin Friendly. Don't take the job here."

She froze and his stomach sank. "Oh. That." She stepped away from his door and he stuck a foot in it so he wouldn't have to wrestle with the key again. "Well, it's a good position, a good group of people, and the manatees. . . ."

He knew she loved manatees. And since they weren't found in Smugglers Cove—or anywhere north of Florida for that matter—that was the one thing Dolphin Friendly couldn't offer her.

"Still," he said, looking for the words to make her stay. "Dolphin Friendly is expanding. There'll be those new boats soon, assuming we get the grants, and then who knows what? New people, new projects—just think of it!" When she shook her head and turned towards her own door, he called after her, "Will you think about it? Please?"

She turned back. "Things are changing at Dolphin Friendly, Smitty. You know it and I know it. It's time for us to recognize that and move on. It's time to grow up. Let's be realistic, pretty soon there'll be nothing really keeping me in the group."

Looking at her, seeing her with both the eyes of a lonely young grad student and the eyes of a grown man who'd only just begun to realize that he was still lonely, he thought she'd never looked more lovely as she did standing barefoot, holding a plastic bucket of melting ice.

"I'm in the group," he said quietly. "And if things are changing, we need to make sure they're changing for the better. Besides, Brody would miss you." Smitty figured that had to be worth something. He wanted to make some sort of sweeping declaration of his feelings—even though he wasn't even sure what they were anymore—but she hadn't wanted to hear them ten years ago, and he was sure she didn't want to hear them now. So he grinned and said, "Come on, Vi. We've been pals for a lot longer than we were girlfriend and boyfriend. Can't we keep it that way?"

He thought he saw a flash of pain in her eyes. Her lips turned up wryly at the corners and she shook her head. "That's exactly the point. We're pals. Let's keep it that way."

With that, she let herself into her room and closed the door.

Smitty stood in the hallway for a long time, wondering exactly what he had missed.

Chapter Nine

"Careful, careful! Don't bang the crate around. This isn't a case full of frozen fish, you know!" Chaz waved his arms wildly as the crane operator goosed the winch too quickly.

Jasper emitted a startled "Hork!" as the compact car-sized crate he was in swung ponderously through the air and bounced off the side of the refrigerator truck.

"Hey, watch it!" Violet—who had been standing near the open doors at the back of the truck—dove for cover as the crate whistled overhead. If Jasper weighed about twelve-hundred pounds, and the crate another thousand . . . she didn't want to think about the damage the two could do together. The poor guy was probably frightened out of his head!

"Put it down!" Smitty waved furiously at the crane operator, who finally played out enough line to set the crate gently on the ground.

"Is he okay?" Chaz asked worriedly, and Violet glanced into the crate.

Jasper's eyes were bright and he was bobbing his head enthusiastically. When he saw Violet, he greeted her with a happy "Hork, hork, hoooork!"

She laughed. "He thinks he's on a carnival ride. I'm pretty sure he just said *higher, faster!*"

Smitty shuddered. He hopped down from one giant caterpillar crane tread and walked over to inspect the side of the truck. "Not much damage, but can we try to keep it that way? Brody'll have my head if we end up owning a dented fifteen-year-old refrigerator truck."

The concept was simple—load Jasper into his traveling crate and use the crane to place the crate on the hydraulic lift at the back of the truck. Because of the high moats surrounding the sea lion arena, and the fact that the fork truck that usually moved the crates around was out of commission, this had seemed the best plan. Now Violet wasn't so sure.

"Okay, one more try." Smitty hopped back up to confer with the crane operator. The big engine motored up, the cable grew tight once again, and the crate was lifted—gently—into the air.

Violet engaged the hydraulic tailgate and waited near the back deck of the truck. The lift was enough to stabilize the ton-plus load and slide it into the truck, but not enough to bring the load up by itself. They were trying to coordinate the crane and the lift together. In theory, it would work.

But in theory, it should've worked the last six tries too.

"I should've been a horse trainer," she muttered to herself as the crate descended towards the lift.

"Why's that?" asked perky Candi.

"Because horses know how to load themselves on trucks," Violet answered shortly. She might not have liked the other woman when she'd been hanging on Smitty's arm the night before, and she certainly hadn't liked her when Smitty had reeled back to his room near midnight, smelling like chocolate perfume, but Violet had to admit that Candi was doing her job now. The blond was in charge of keeping Jasper cool and happy while he was being loaded. She had a hose with a spray nozzle, and was wetting the sea lion down regularly as well as feeding him small pieces of fish now and again to keep him thinking this was all fun and games.

Sea lions, like most marine mammals, overheated easily—with disastrous consequences.

"Okay, bring it down now," Violet called and waved her arm for the crane operator to start lowering Jasper's crate.

Besides, she thought, Candi wasn't the problem. Smitty was the problem. If he didn't see her as anything more than a "pal"—and he'd made that pretty clear the night before—then there really wasn't any hope for them, was there?

Violet wasn't sure when she started thinking that there might be hope for the two of them. It was probably when she'd played with that little boy at the water park and thought how much she'd wanted children, once upon a time. That was right about the time she realized that if she and Smitty tried another relationship and it failed, then one of them would have to leave Dolphin Friendly.

Then when Chaz had made his offer, she began to wonder whether it might just be better to avoid the inevitable heartbreak all together and switch jobs now.

Cowardice, maybe. But it was the safe, painless option. She glanced at Smitty and her heart turned over in her chest. Okay, she amended. Maybe just the less painful option.

"Are we still on target?" The shout returned her attention to the descent of the heavy crate, and through a combination of fair winds, clear skies, and general dumb luck they managed to drop Jasper squarely on the hydraulic lift this time.

There was a ragged chorus of cheers from the Seaquarium staff, and a general sigh of relief when the crate slid into the refrigerator truck without further incident. A few of the trainers waved or shed a quiet tear as Violet shut the doors on Jasper's last sight of sunny Florida.

"He'll be okay in Boston, won't he?" Candi's lower lip trembled as she looked to Violet for reassurance.

"Er—" Violet backed away a step. "Sure, he'll be fine. The trainers at the Boston Aquarium are topnotch. Good people."

"Thanks," Candi whispered. Her big blue eyes filled with tears. "I'll just miss him so much. He's such a good boy." She launched herself against Violet and clung, crying hiccuppy sobs.

Violet struggled to free herself without being too obvious. She patted the blond's heaving shoulder with one hand while waving frantically for help with the other. She glanced up for rescue, and saw Smitty standing nearby, grinning. She mouthed *Get her off me!* and he shook his head. He knew full well that emotions—particularly female ones—worried her to no end.

"Come on darling, it'll be okay," Chaz came to

the rescue, peeling Candi off Violet and handing the sobbing blond over to another staffer. "Jasper will make lots of new friends in Boston."

He shook his head and grinned as Candi was led away, sniffling. To Violet, he said, "I promise if you come work with me that I won't let her hug you more than once a month." He grinned at her shudder. "And I won't assign her to your team, okay?" He passed her a card, which was almost blown away when Smitty started the truck's engine and revved it until it belched a black cloud all over Chaz.

Violet suppressed a smile when her one-time partner in crime leaned his head out of the cab and called a completely false, "Sorry!"

Chaz pulled her away from the vehicle and tapped the card. "Here are the numbers where you can reach me. I'm serious about the offer."

She nodded and didn't glance over when Smitty revved the truck again. "I'm seriously thinking about it. You said housing was included?" She thought about the years she'd spent with Dolphin Friendly, either sleeping onboard in a hammock because they couldn't afford a hotel, or staying in those crummy apartments they rented by the week. Then she thought of her pretty room at Smugglers Cove, and the view of the ocean she had out her window. About the curtains and bedspread she and Maddy were going to shop for when she got home.

Except it might not be home for long.

"Yes," Chaz replied. "Housing is included."

"Would I get my own closet?"

He laughed. "You'd get your own condo." He put his hand on her back and steered her to the front of the truck, opened her door for her, and handed her up. "Think about it and get back to me after the opening ceremony. I want to flesh out the new team by the end of the month."

Smitty slammed the transmission into reverse before Chaz even got the door shut, forcing him to jump out of the way as the truck lurched backwards, spun around, and accelerated away from Seaquarium Florida.

Violet couldn't help laughing. "That was rude. Wouldn't you have felt bad if you'd run his toes over?"

Smitty shook his head and grinned. "Not really. Besides, we need to get old Jasper up to Smugglers Cove by noon tomorrow, so there's no time to stand around chitchatting, is there?" When she drew in a breath to reply, he glanced at the now-empty specimen jar. "Should we put our money in now or later?"

She let the breath back out on a wistful sigh. "Let's not. We've declared a truce, right? I'd like to drive home without fighting, if we can manage it." It came to her that this could very well be the last time she and Smitty were really alone together. If Chaz was serious about putting the team together inside of a month, she'd have to leave Dolphin Friendly sooner rather than later.

"Well, if you don't want to fight, what do you want to do? Talk? Play a game?"

She glanced over at his profile and had to stop herself from touching the line of his jaw where the stubble showed a burnished red. She took the easy way out. "I think I'm going to take a nap. Wake me up when it's my turn to drive."

He woke her up sooner than that, shaking her gently as he eased the truck onto the shoulder of the road. "Vi. Come on, wake up. We've got a problem."

Nervous twinges flickered through him as he glanced yet again at the gauge on the dash. The little orange arrow should've pointed towards one of the cool blue numbers. It had all the way out of Florida.

Now it was reading in the orange. He shook Violet again and set the parking brake.

"Huh? Wha—?" She woke up slowly at first, then snapped to attention when she realized they were stopped on the side of the highway. "What's wrong? We get a flat?"

"Nope. Worse. The refrigerator quit and Jasper's area is heating up fast."

"Oh, no!" She beat him to the back of the truck. They opened the doors together and immediately felt that the air inside the lit refrigerator compartment wasn't much colder than outside.

"Hork?" Jasper didn't seem uncomfortable yet, but Smitty knew that the border between a happy sea lion and a broiled sea lion was a fine line.

"Grab the water jugs and let's wet him down." Matching action to words, Violet hopped into the truck and uncapped one of the bluc water jugs they'd loaded in for just such an emergency. Smitty did the same, then he examined the interior of the cargo area, hoping for a miracle.

"No windows we can open to give him a breeze. Guess the designers didn't have live transport in mind when they put this truck together." He glanced outside at the midday southern sunlight. "It's only going to get hotter in here, but we can't wait around for a repair. Not if we want to be back in Smugglers Cove in time for the ceremony."

Violet nodded. "Let's get back on the road. You can make some calls and line up a repairman to meet us along the way. We can ice him down if necessary, but we've got to keep his body temp down."

They closed the doors on a slightly warm-looking sea lion. "Think he'll be okay?" Smitty asked dubiously as Violet pulled herself into the driver's seat.

She nodded. "He'd better be, or we'll be in worse trouble with Brody than we were when we left Smugglers Cove. What do you think is wrong with the refrigerator?"

"Dunno." Smitty shrugged. "There's a reason we've always kept a dedicated mechanic on staff. I'm hopeless with this sort of thing, and you're even worse. At least *I've* never filled the pickup's radiator with oil."

He grinned when she spluttered. Score one for him. Now, if he could just figure out how to keep Jasper cool, he'd be ahead of the game. He flipped the cell phone open, took a card of emergency numbers out of his wallet, and started making calls as the truck pulled back onto the highway.

It was going to be a long evening.

"When did we stop last?" Smitty asked, glancing back down at the temp gauge, which was staying stubbornly in the orange.

Violet glanced at her watch. "Two hours ago. We should stop again soon and buy more ice. The hundred pounds we bought at the last place is probably almost gone by now."

Smitty grunted and nodded. He'd been worried when his calls had proven that there was no such thing as roadside refrigerator repair—at least not on

I-95 north. But Jasper seemed to be holding his own, and it was dusk now, so the outside temperature should drop soon.

Brody had taken the news remarkably well, only threatening to fire them both if anything happened to Jasper. Then he'd told them to be careful, wished them luck, and threatened to fire them again if they didn't get to Smugglers Cove by noon the next day.

Smitty thought philosophically that being fired might not be such a bad thing. He'd been thinking that if Violet decided to leave Dolphin Friendly, he might go as well. Things just wouldn't be the same without her.

"There! Pull over there." Violet pointed across the road.

There was a small building with two tired-looking gas pumps out front and a faded cola sign above the door. It wasn't impressive, but it was the first convenience store they'd seen in a half hour. This would've been surprising if they were still on the main road, but Smitty had elected to take one of the bypasses listed in the map to avoid the last big city. Unfortunately, they hadn't actually made it back to I-95 yet, which limited their ice choices.

"Got it." He pulled up to a pump, figuring he'd top off the gas while they were at it. There was no telling how much longer they'd be on the bypass.

Violet had been a surprisingly good sport about the detour, but there was no way she'd let him live it down if they ran out of gas. Not to mention the fact that Jasper couldn't stand the delay. If anything happened to the borrowed sea lion, Smitty wouldn't be worried about Violet letting him live it down. He'd be worried about Brody letting him live. Period.

When the gas tank was full, Smitty followed Violet into the little store.

"What do you mean you don't have any ice?" he heard her ask the grandmotherly woman behind the counter. Loudly.

Smitty's stomach sank. "Uh-oh. No ice?"

The woman behind the counter—whose name tag proclaimed that she was Flo—shook her head. "Sorry kids. The ice maker broke a week ago and we're still waiting on a part. You need it for a party or something?"

Violet muttered, "Or something," and stalked over to the freezer cases at the back of the store.

Smitty tried his best grin. "Is there another store between here and I-95 that might have a hundred pounds or so of ice available?"

Even before he finished the question, Flo was shaking her head. "No other store on this road for another hour at least. There's a place a half hour back the way you came that might have some, though."

"Can't do that." Violet had come up behind him when he wasn't looking. It made him jumpy when she did that. Like he wasn't jumpy enough at the thought of Jasper getting sick under his and Violet's care. She glanced pointedly at her watch and continued, "We'd miss the opening ceremonies. This 'bypass' has made us late enough already."

She was right, but he didn't have to like it. She walked back toward the freezer cases and he followed, snapping, "Well then, what do you suggest? We're not going to gain any points by showing up on time with a sick performing sea lion, are we?"

"We won't." She grinned smugly and held up a package of frozen peas. "We'll ice his cage down with frozen food. It should do the trick."

He stared at her.

Violet squirmed and tried to hide the peas behind her back. "It's the dumbest idea you've ever heard, right?"

Smitty shook his head. "No. It's brilliant. I just forget sometimes how smart you are."

"Thanks a lot." She made a face, but he could tell she was pleased.

Thinking of the limit on the Dolphin Friendly credit card, he nodded. "It should work, as long as we keep him from eating the food."

She'd already thought of that. "Double wrap the

stuff in garbage bags before we lay them on the top and sides of the crate. He won't get the bonus of cold water dripping on him like he did with the ice bags, but it's better than letting him cook for another hour, right?"

He nodded. "Right." He grabbed a shopping cart—one of only two in the store—and loaded it up with the contents of the double freezers at the end of the little room. Pizzas, ice cream, frozen corn, pop-up biscuits, Popsicles, and frozen French fries all went into the cart. Flo's eyes had nearly popped out of their sockets by the time both shopping carts were loaded with every frozen item in the store.

And three boxes of garbage bags.

The shopkeeper rang it all up without comment, only faltering a little when Violet added a big bag of cheez puffs, a six-pack of cola, and a women's magazine to the tab.

Smitty paid with the card and borrowed the carts to tote their purchases out to the truck. On the way out the door, he called over his shoulder, "And Flo? Can we borrow that garden hose outside for a few minutes?"

The woman nodded, and as the door shut behind him, Smitty thought he heard her say, "Must be some strange sort of party they're planning."

He snorted. Violet snickered. He darted a glance

at her, saw her eyes swimming with merriment, then looked at the mound of frozen food they'd bought, crowned by a six-pack of soda and a magazine with the headline *Honesty in Your Relationship? Take Our Quiz!*

He snorted again. She giggled. They looked at each other and broke down completely, howling with laughter and gasping out little bits of information that sent them back into gales of mirth.

"Did you see the look on—" She giggled.

"Her face! She thought we were having some sort of—" Smitty couldn't finish. He was laughing too hard.

"Party!" they howled in unison, and had to hold each other up.

He leaned on one of the carts and tried to catch a breath, but the cart rolled away, starting a small avalanche of "pizza for one" and microwave mac and cheese boxes that set them off laughing again.

"Hey babe, wanna party?" Smitty grabbed Violet by the waist and swung her around in a big circle while they both laughed. "I'll bring the frozen corn and the cheez puffs—"

"And I'll bring a hundred fifty black garbage bags," she finished, giggling. She wrapped her arms around his neck and probably intended to give him a friendly kiss on the cheek. But the devil inside him made Smitty turn his face just in time, making their lips touch for the first time in ten years.

They froze. Lip to lip. Eye to eye. Nose to nose.

And Smitty heard something go *click* in his head. In his heart.

Their laughter died. Something else was born, something soft and needy, warm and greedy. Violet took her hands from around his neck, put them on his chest—

And shoved.

He stumbled back a pace, bumped into the other shopping cart and sent it rolling down the gentle slope to the road. By the time he'd snagged the cart, Violet was pushing the other load towards the refrigerator truck.

"Come on, Smits," she called over her shoulder in a perfectly normal voice, as though the world hadn't just tilted on its axis. "Let's get this stuff packed around Jasper and be on our way."

He caught up to her as she was opening the back doors of the truck. He touched her arm. "Vi?"

She moved away from him. "Jasper still looks okay. You want to get Flo's hose and wet him down while I start packing garbage bags with the frozen stuff?"

"Vi, about what just happened—"

She interrupted him. "Don't worry about it. My

lips slipped. It happens. Doesn't mean a thing." She ripped open one of the boxes and started pulling out black plastic bags. "It never happened, okay?"

No, it's not okay. I want it to have happened. I want it to happen again. Smitty felt like yelling at the top of his lungs. Then he realized that what he *really* felt like yelling was, *How can you possibly think about leaving Dolphin Friendly? Leaving me?*

"Smitty? The hose?" She couldn't quite meet his eyes, but he knew from experience that pushing her now would get him exactly nowhere. He gritted his teeth.

"Sure. Fine." He stomped off to get the hose because she was right, they didn't have time to hash this out now. But as he passed the little pile of snacks and soda she'd left on the hood of the truck, the magazine headline caught his eye, and he had an idea. He only hoped it was a good one, because he was starting to feel like he was running out of time.

Or, more precisely, like he and Violet were running out of time.

Chapter Ten

Violet waited until he'd gone before she let out a shaky breath and pressed a hand to her chest. Her heart was still rocketing along on the beat it had chosen when she and Smitty had kissed.

Honestly, it hadn't been much of a kiss. More like a handshake, only with lips. A lipshake. It hadn't been passionate. Hadn't involved more than fleeting contact.

So why were her hands trembling?

"Hork?"

She shook her head. "I don't know, Jasper. Everything's so complicated all of a sudden. He doesn't want me. I don't *want* him to want me. That would

135

ruin everything we've both worked so hard for." The sea lion bobbed his head in commiseration and she noticed that the skin around his throat seemed looser. She pinched a little bit between her thumb and forefinger and it snapped back quickly enough that she wasn't too worried. But she thought he was getting a little dehydrated. "We'd better get you on the road, huh?"

"Hork, hork."

She doubled up on the bags and started filling them with frozen food. "We'll get back to the main highway and it should only take us another eighteen hours or so to get to Smugglers Cove. Then you can do your stuff at the opening ceremonies. . . ." She trailed off.

Then what?

"Flo's watching us through the window with a cordless phone jammed to her ear," Smitty announced when he returned with the hose. "Wonder what she's telling the neighbors?" He grinned and she wondered whether she'd imagined that he'd been affected by their kiss. He seemed normal enough now—well, as normal as Smitty ever got.

Maybe it was all one-sided.

She scowled. "We're late and getting later. I'm almost done with our freezer bags, so turn the hose on him and let's get out of here."

He snapped a smart salute. "Aye-aye, Captain Oliver. Hose ahoy."

"Don't be an idiot," she said, but she found her lips stretching into a grin.

Somehow, even when things seemed at their worst, he made her smile.

They got back on the road quickly after that, and with Violet driving, they reached I-95 in under an hour. Smitty's shortcut had added two hours onto their journey and he was profoundly grateful she hadn't mentioned it. Yet.

Jasper seemed okay when they stopped near the North Carolina line as darkness began to fall. They added some ice to the surprisingly effective garbage-bag cold packs and dined on soggy truck-stop cheeseburgers to go. The jar on the dashboard remained empty. They hadn't fought.

Then again, they hadn't spoken much either.

When the night had closed in around them, and with it had come that numb sort of lethargy that overtakes the human body when it realizes that it's not going to bed that night, Smitty clicked on his flashlight and pulled out the women's magazine.

"What are you doing?" Her voice sounded strange in the cab, maybe because they'd been silent so long.

"Looking for something to keep us awake. The

radio stations around here seem to be our choice between a rerun of yesterday's minor league baseball game and an infomercial on hair plugs. It's a little too dark for a game of 'I Spy,' unless you count 'I spy a dark shadow over there next to that big black thing,' which I don't. We're pretty much alone on the road, which makes the 'license plate game' a little irrelevant. And I don't get the impression you're in the mood for small talk. So I thought we could try this relationship quiz in the magazine you bought. Just for fun."

He held his breath, waiting for her answer. He'd skimmed the quiz earlier when she'd been checking on Jasper, and he thought his plan might work.

"We're not in a relationship," she pointed out unnecessarily.

"Sure we are," he replied. "Not necessarily in the way the magazine probably means, but we see each other every day. Our rooms at the inn are down the hall from each other, for goodness' sake. That's closer than a lot of people in real relationships, right?"

"I still can't believe you ended up with the private bathroom in your room," Violet grumped irrelevantly.

"Don't change the subject. Do you want to try it or not?"

They drove in silence for a moment, passing a town line that quickly receded in the distance. Then she shrugged. "Sure, why not."

Grinning in the darkness, he aimed his flashlight at the magazine and read the introduction to the quiz, adapting it only slightly for his own purposes. "It says here that first off we both have to agree to tell only the truth when answering the questions, even if we're afraid it might hurt the other person's feelings."

She snickered. "Since when have I been afraid of hurting your feelings?"

That brought a few comments to mind, but Smitty let it slide. He continued. "And there's no such thing as a pass, or pleading the Fifth, or anything. We each have to come up with an answer to every question."

The truck labored to climb a gentle hill, and she downshifted before answering. "Fine. Anything else?" She was starting to sound intrigued.

"Nope, that's it. Question one." He read by flashlight beam, hoping the jiggling light and the small print wouldn't make him carsick. "Name one thing you don't like about the other person."

"Ooh, I'm having fun already." Violet paused. "Do I have to pick just one?"

"That's what it says."

"Okay, well then . . ." They drove in silence while

she thought, and Smitty shifted nervously, wondering what horrible list of crimes was parading through her head. But when she spoke again, her voice was surprised. "Actually, that's a tough question. The stuff that annoys me is part of what makes you Smitty, you know? How about you go first while I think? What one thing don't you like about me?"

Because he'd skimmed the questions earlier, he had an answer ready. "I don't like that you run away when things get tough."

She drew in a breath, stung. "That's not fair. I do not run away! I stuck with Dolphin Friendly through the lean years, and you can say that so quickly? Thanks a lot!" She pressed her lips together, clearly insulted that he'd answered so fast. She sniffed. "I don't think I want to play anymore."

"See? You're ready to quit already. But I don't mean that you run away from tough stuff at work. It's the emotional stuff. When things start getting heavy, you take off, or change the subject, or start a fight, or take a nap. That's what I'm talking about."

"I'm not running now," she pointed out.

"Only because you're driving a truck that's doing sixty miles an hour and we can't stop because we're late. Yes?"

She didn't dignify that with a response. Then she said, "Fine. I don't like how you're always on the edge of things, always second in command. I think you should try putting your own butt on the line sometime instead of hiding behind Brody."

Ouch. Somehow when he'd hatched his plan, Smitty hadn't thought about the fact that they'd be lobbing live ammunition at each other. He'd intended to use the quiz to get them talking to each other and maybe ease her into thinking about taking another shot at a relationship with him. The plan hadn't been for them to spend the rest of the drive trying to score points off each other.

"Maybe this wasn't such a good idea after all," he muttered as he flipped a couple of pages and glanced at the rest of the questions.

"Now who's running? Hit me with the next question."

"Okay, you asked for it. It's the reverse of the last one. Name one thing you like about the other person, and you have to go first this time because I went first before."

They passed into Virginia and Violet glanced at a bright yellow sign. "There's a Travelers' Aid truck stop twenty miles up the road. Want to stop and change Jasper's ice when we get there?"

"Fine, but no stalling. Name one thing you like about me."

She blew out a frustrated breath and made a face

like she'd just eaten a sour olive. "Though I hate to admit it, I like almost everything about you, Smits, one way or another. That's why—"

"Why what?"

"Never mind."

Though he wanted to push, Smitty settled back in the uncomfortable passenger's seat. " 'Everything' doesn't count as an answer. You've got to name one thing."

"Urg. Fine," she snapped. "I like that you don't get really angry, even when things are going completely wrong around you. You're like an island of calmness sometimes. I like that."

"Hmm," he said, enjoying the image. "An island of calmness. . . ."

"Don't let it go to your head," she cautioned. "I'll deny I said that if you ever repeat it. Now, your turn. Tell me what you like about me, and make it good."

He grinned. "I like that you've been helping Maddy with her hair and you don't want anyone to know about it. I think it's really sweet."

She groaned. "Sweet? Ick. And the only reason I'm doing it is because I got tired of seeing frizzy curls across the breakfast table. Besides, how do you know about it anyway?"

"A little fish told me." Smitty chuckled and skipped a couple of questions he didn't think applied to the two of them like the one about backseats of cars and the one about whipped cream. Geez, the things these magazines came up with. Finally, he said, "Next question. What's the best day of your life?"

"You're first," she reminded him.

He hadn't been able to think of a good answer for this one, but he'd been curious to see what she would say. He thought a moment. "I guess most people would say the day they graduated, or the day they got married." Violet stiffened when he said the 'm' word. "But I guess I'd have to say the first day we met the dolphins off Smugglers Point. Remember it? Brody had taken the Zodiac back to the inn because he was so gaga over Maddy he couldn't be away from her, and we stayed out with the interns because the humpbacks were singing."

Violet smiled, remembering. "You and I dove down to hear the whales sing. There was a mother and a calf."

"Yeah, and the song was all around us and the dolphins were playing nearby, and then we saw that little pod of right whales." Smitty remembered the wonder of it all. Ten years after he'd started his career in the water, and he could still be humbled by the beauty of the Great Whales. "There are what? Three hundred right whales in the Atlantic? And we saw five of 'em that day."

"I'd never seen an Atlantic right whale before," Violet said, remembering, and to Smitty it seemed as though the cab of the truck was briefly filled with the gurgle of air being expelled from his regulator and the sound of the singing humpbacks.

"It was a good day," he said.

"The best."

They fell silent, each remembering the moment. Remembering that they'd been together. He broke the quiet. "So what's your best day?"

"I guess I'll have to go for next best, because otherwise I'd have to second your vote, which is probably cheating." She took a breath, "I'd say the day we saved that group of pilot whales."

"Ah yes," Smitty agreed with a happy sigh. "That was an excellent day."

Brody had been on a brief lecture tour when Violet and Smitty had gotten the call. Six pilot whales ranging in length from eight to twenty feet had chased a school of mackerel into a shallow harbor. The tide had turned and a sandbar loomed between the whales and open ocean. They would be stranded in one hour. Dead in six.

"I still can't believe you talked the city council into okaying that trench," Smitty said, still amazed by the memory.

She grinned. "I merely pointed out that six decaying

pilot whales weren't going to add to their upcoming Harbor Arts Festival, nor would banners explaining how they sentenced helpless marine mammals to death because they didn't want their sandbar messed with."

"And besides," Smitty remembered, "after the teenage chain gang you assembled dug out the trench and we herded the whales to safety, we filled it in good as new."

"More or less. I wasn't really that worried about the sandbar." Violet smiled. "I just wanted to save the whales. Anyway, it was a good day."

"The best." He repeated her earlier words, and a sense of contentment stole over the cab.

"Here's the truck stop," she said as they passed another sign. "Want to read the next question before we pull in, so we can be thinking about our answers?" She downshifted and signaled before easing the truck onto the off-ramp.

When he didn't answer right away, she glanced over. "What?"

"Haven't you guessed the next question? They come in pairs."

"Oh." She pulled into the truck lot and killed the engine, set the parking brake, and asked the question for both of them.

"What was your worst day?"

Chapter Eleven

"How many bags of ice?"

Violet rolled her eyes at the clerk behind the counter. "A hundred. Do you have that many?"

"What do you need with that much ice?" The kid couldn't have been more than twenty, but he winked as if to say, *Don't worry, baby. I can take care of a pretty little thing like you.*

Feeling raw from the impromptu soul baring that had taken place in the truck, and too tired to go through the usual *I'm having a party, wink, wink, nudge, nudge* routine, she snapped, "Because I have a twelve-hundred-pound trained sea lion outside in a refrigerator truck that's not refrigerating, and if I don't keep him cool between here and Cape Cod then he could very well die. Okay? Do you have a hundred bags of ice or not?"

While the youth stammered that they only had fifty bags of ice on-hand at any given time, Violet felt a tap on her shoulder. She spun, figuring Smitty had snuck up on her again.

It was a stranger with a baseball cap and a neatly trimmed moustache. "I couldn't help overhearing, ma'am, but did you say you've got a sea lion overheating in a 'fridge truck outside?"

"Yes. Yes, I do, and no, you can't meet the sea lion." She pressed a hand to her eyes, trying to stave off the headache that seemed inevitable.

Smitty had come up beside her during the exchange, and handed her a cup of coffee. She swigged it gratefully.

"What Violet meant to say was 'yes, we have a sea lion in a broken refrigerator truck outside.' " Smitty nudged her and she nodded at Mr. Moustache.

"Sorry," she said. "I'm a little stressed."

The stranger nodded. "Understandable. The reason I asked, though, is because I've worked on a few of those trucks in my time. Maybe I can help with the cooling unit."

Quicker than he could say 'moustache,' they whisked the man out to the truck, where he gave the old refrigeration unit a checkup. He muttered a few things while he tinkered, then went to his own truck and returned with a small toolbox.

"This thing get banged around recently? You have an accident or something?" the man—whose name was Roy—asked as he fiddled with the compressor's guts.

"No. No accident," Smitty answered, just as Violet said, "Yes, the unit was hit by a flying sea lion crate several times while we were trying to load it."

"A flying . . . ? Never mind," Roy said. "You knocked one of the hoses out of its fitting. I've got it cobbled back together now. Start 'er up and let's see what happens."

Violet started 'er up and the unit chattered to life. She heard cheers from outside. It seemed that they had attracted something of a crowd. She supposed it wasn't every day that a sea lion visited the Travelers' Assistance truck stop.

Cheered by the success of the repair, and just starting to think everything was going to be okay, she jumped back onto the pavement just in time to hear a squawk from Smitty. "Violet!"

She saw that the doors at the back of the truck were open, and her heart sank to her stomach. She sprinted back, yelling, "What's wrong? Should I call a vet?"

Not that the local cat and cow vet would be much help if Jasper was overheating.

But Jasper wasn't overheating. It was better than that. And in a way, worse.

She skidded to a stop and stared. Whitish goo oozed out of the back of the truck and fell with a plop onto the dark pavement. The interior light of the refrigerator compartment wasn't great, but it was enough to illuminate Smitty's form next to Jasper's crate. Smitty was holding a limp torn piece of black plastic. More of the white glop dribbled from it.

"Hork, hork!" Jasper bobbed his head and then, incredibly, belched. Instead of looking dry and over-heated like she might have expected, he looked wet and vaguely . . . slimy.

"What happened?" Violet squeaked, aware that the crowd of truckers had pressed closer to see Jasper.

"I think . . ." Smitty's voice sounded funny, like he wasn't sure whether to laugh, cry, or run screaming. "I think he ate through one of the bags. Or two." Another blob fell. "Or all of them."

Violet's gaze landed on a chunk floating in the white goo. It looked like a half-eaten pepperoni pizza. The goo could've been melted ice cream. The slime on Jasper's back could be liquefied Popsicles. "Oh man. Brody's going to kill us. We've fed an entire freezer case to the sea lion."

Jasper burped again.

"Can seals eat pepperoni?" called a voice from the crowd.

"He's a sea lion, not a seal," Violet replied, shutting the doors on Smitty and Jasper. "And you can ask me about the pepperoni tomorrow. I'll probably know by then." She thanked Roy profusely, got in the truck, and drove to the truck wash at the back of the lot.

They had a half hour to wash away the incriminating evidence and get back on the road. Then they could only pray that sea lions actually *could* eat pepperoni. And ice cream. And popsicles.

Every hour from Virginia to Maryland, they pulled over and checked on Jasper. Each time, he greeted them with a cheerful 'Hork!' and a flipper wave. The truck had cooled right down now that the compressor was working, the cargo area had been washed out thoroughly, and home was getting closer by the mile.

So why was she feeling, if possible, even more on edge than she had been before?

"You ready to keep going on that quiz now that we seem to be on the right track with Jasper and the truck?"

She glanced at Smitty. *That* was why she was edgy. That last question. "I'm not sure I'm still in the mood for that silliness, okay Smits? Let's just head home and forget about the quiz."

His soft chuckle carried over the hum of the engine. "Running again, Vi?"

"I'm not running," she snapped. "I'm . . . Oh, fine. I'll answer the darn question. Then can we toss that magazine out the window, please?"

"No littering," he said mildly. "And the question was to name your worst day."

She thought a moment. Just as her best day had been with Smitty, her worst day had been with him also. Or rather, without him. "I thought about picking that day at the water park when you asked me to make a family with you. Or the day I found out you were marrying Ellen. Or the day you actually did." Smitty shifted in the passenger's seat as the list grew long. "But I think my worst day was the day I left the Puget Sound Project and came back to Dolphin Friendly."

"Was it such a bad choice then? Do you wish you'd stayed with . . . Chaz?" he asked quietly.

She turned and thought she saw real pain in his eyes. She shook her head. "Don't be silly. I love Dolphin Friendly and I wouldn't trade the last eight years for anything."

"Then why are you going to leave?"

He said that like it was a foregone conclusion.

Like she'd already given her notice. The idea made Violet sad. She stared into darkness that was marked only by a dashed line on the open highway. "Do you want to know why that's my worst day or not?"

"Go ahead."

She took a breath. "When Brody wrote and told me that you and Ellen had divorced, I was glad. Not because I wanted you to hurt—though maybe that was part of it—but because I thought it meant there was still a chance for the two of us. So I quit Puget Sound and came home to Dolphin Friendly."

"We were all waiting for you on the dock," he remembered, his voice hoarse.

"Yes. You and Brody and a couple of interns I'd never met. Brody hugged me. The interns shook my hand. And you faded into the background. After two years, you barely even said 'hello.' "

She felt that unfamiliar burn in her eyes and told herself it wasn't time to cry now. Maybe after she'd given her notice, she'd lock the door and let the tears come—but not until then.

"What did you expect?" he asked as though truly surprised. "We'd drifted apart even before you left. And you'd turned down my proposal. How was I supposed to know you were expecting flowers and a marching band?"

"Don't make a joke of this," she snapped. "Of

course I didn't want a parade." Her voice softened. "I just wanted you to hug me and say you were sorry. Then I could say I was sorry and we could go from there. But we never did that."

"No, we didn't." His voice seemed to come out of the darkness. She felt him take her hand where it rested on the gearshift. She didn't pull away.

"You want to hear about my worst day?" he asked quietly.

She nodded.

"My worst day was the day my mother died."

Violet was surprised. She'd expected him to say his worst day was at the water park in California, the day he married Ellen, or the day she divorced him. But though her own parents were alive and well in the Midwest, surrounded by her landlocked siblings, she imagined that she might consider it her worst day if one of them died unexpectedly.

"You didn't know me before she died," Smitty said. It was true, they'd met at U.C. Santa Cruz when school started in the fall. His mother had died that summer. He continued, "So you didn't understand how much it had affected me."

They were driving into a storm, and the first fat raindrops hit the windshield. Violet slowed down and turned on the wipers. "You talked about her sometimes. You loved her very much. I always felt a little guilty because I had such a big family and you . . . didn't."

"It was more than just missing her, though there was some of that," he said. "It was the feeling of being all alone. Nobody cared what my grades were anymore. Nobody was going to nag me to go to the dentist once a year or call me on Sundays just to chat." He rubbed a hand across his face and Violet heard the auburn stubble rasp across the calluses on his palm.

Unaccountably, she found herself growing irritated with him. "Didn't it matter to you that we were together that fall? *I* cared what your grades were—at least enough to make sure I was beating you in at least half our classes. *I* cared whether you went to the dentist. *I* called to chat with you. Brody did too." She knew it wasn't the same thing, but it still stung. *She had cared.* How dare he make it seem like it wasn't enough?

She frowned as the truck hurtled through the rainy night and crossed into Pennsylvania.

She'd loved him. Had it really meant so little?

Apparently. He shrugged and said, "I'm not saying I was right, but at the time I thought I needed more. I needed to have someone I believed was going to care about those things for the rest of our lives." He paused. "Remember that trip we took on the *Outreach*?"

"Of course. It was our first real taste of open ocean fieldwork, and it was almost a disaster when that squall came up. Brody was washed over the side and you went in after him. For a minute there we couldn't see either of you."

Violet shuddered with the remembered chill. She had never been so terrified before or since. For several minutes, they'd all thought Brody and Smitty were both lost. How had that memory been supplanted by the black days that followed it? She hadn't thought of *Outreach* in years.

"Well, that scared me silly. I realized that if I'd drowned that day, there was nothing to prove I ever existed." Smitty squeezed her hand. Violet was surprised to find him still holding it. "And the next day you and I went to the water park and I made a hash of proposing to you and not listening to why you said no. I was so caught up in the idea of having someone who was legally obligated to care whether I came home from every voyage, I lost track that there was someone else involved in the equation. You. I think I was even a little glad you said no, because I knew you were going to be out on the water with me—and what if something happened to you? Then I'd be alone again."

Violet sniffed. "I'm not finding this explanation particularly heartwarming." But in a way she was. It hadn't really been about her, even back then. She could still hate him for being foolish, but she couldn't totally blame him.

"I'm just trying to tell you about my worst day, and how it led to a string of bad decisions I'm still trying to recover from." He paused. "So anyway, I'm sorry. I was so caught up in being all alone in the world that I ended up hurting the one person in the world I loved. The one person who wanted to be there for me. You were the best thing that ever happened to me, Vi, and I blew it."

Now the tears were threatening in earnest. Violet felt one slide down the side of her face and brushed it away on the pretext of scratching her cheek. "Would've been nice if you'd said all that when I got back from Puget Sound." Her voice broke and she hated him for what he could still make her feel. He accused her of running away from other people's emotions? This was why. He'd taught her well that emotions could only hurt.

"Yeah, well. I still had some growing up to do. You said the other day that we were both too young and too stupid to have made it work back then, and you're probably right. But still, I wish it could've been different. I wish Ma hadn't died that summer. I wish you and I had met at a different time in my life. I wish it had ended differently between us."

Ended.

And there it was. As far as Smitty was concerned, it was over between them. They were pals. Buddies. Friends. There was no going back, no going forward.

Violet sniffed and wiped her cheek again. "Are there any more questions in this dumb quiz?"

He didn't flick the flashlight on to check, and she wondered whether he was reciting from memory or asking the question he wanted to know when he said, "If you could have one wish granted, what would it be?"

"You first."

He shook his head. "Nope. I'm changing the rules. You first."

She didn't argue.

I wish we could try again, she wanted to yell. *I wish we could go back and do it all over.* But she couldn't say that. She'd look foolish. Desperate. Like she was clinging to the memory of a relationship that was, by his own words, ended.

The rules had said she couldn't edit her answers to save the other person's feelings. They hadn't said anything about her own.

So when she answered, she intentionally lied to Smitty for the first time in their rocky ten-year friendship. "I wish that the job at Seaquarium is as wonderful as it sounds, that I get to save hundreds of manatees, and I don't give in to the urge to drown the eternally perky Candi."

In the cab of the truck there was silence except for the swish of tires on the wet pavement and the rhythmic thump of the wipers as they dashed the rain aside. A mile marker passed. Another.

Then Smitty said huskily, "Then that's what I wish for too, Violet. I just want you to be happy."

He cleared his throat, threw the flashlight and the magazine in the foot well, and pointed at an exit sign. "Pull off here and let's switch. I need to drive for a while."

Chapter Twelve

Well, that pretty much said it all. Smitty scowled as he sent the truck hurtling into the morning's bloody light. She was leaving Dolphin Friendly and starting a whole new life down in Florida, and nothing he could do was going to change it. She'd as much as said so.

He glanced over. She was sleeping now. He was pretty sure she'd been faking when they first got back on the road—unless she regularly slept with her shoulder muscles bunched, her fists clenched, and her breath hitching. If she'd been any other woman he might've thought she was crying. But hey, this was Violet. She never cried.

Either way, she was asleep now and he was grateful for it. All he wanted to do now was get the heck back to Smugglers Cove, deliver their belching, lactose-intolerant sea lion to Brody's tender mercies, and sleep until it was time for the grand opening gala that evening.

They were somewhere in Connecticut now, and home was feeling closer by the mile. In spite of all their adventures, they would arrive on or near their noon deadline.

Had they really left Smugglers Cove just four short days ago? It seemed like a decade had passed since they'd set off, and Smitty was feeling every one of those years as he downshifted to pass a school bus full of children. He hit the accelerator and sped by, trying to ignore the small, waving hands and laughing mouths.

He kept the pedal down once the bus had disappeared in the distance. It would be good to get home.

"Violet? Come on, Violet. It's time to get up now so you can go sleep in a real bed." She was dimly conscious of gentle hands shaking her, of a female voice talking to her.

"Maddy? What're you doing in Pennsylvania?"

The other woman's laugh tinkled, sounding like

home. "You slept through Pennsylvania, silly. And the rest of the ride. You're in the driveway." Maddy helped Violet out of the truck.

"I never want to sit in another bucket seat as long as I live," Violet croaked as Maddy helped her across the clamshell driveway and into the inn. A feeling of peace descended on her when she stepped into the welcoming front hall.

She was home.

Then she frowned. No, that wasn't right. Home was going to be a condo in Florida. This was only a place she was staying temporarily, before she officially left Dolphin Friendly.

The thought brought an ache that almost stole her breath away.

"How was the ride?" Maddy asked as she and Violet climbed the familiar staircase with its pretty oriental runner.

Violet shrugged, dredging up some of her usual defenses as her head started to clear. "Not bad. Smitty and I talked. A lot." Too much. So much that she finally believed there was nothing left for her here except memories. "It was okay."

Maddy paused outside Violet's door. "Before we go in, I just want you to know that if you don't like it, we can return it and pick out something you like better. I just saw it and thought of you." She shrugged, smiled sheepishly, and opened the door.

Violet stepped over the threshold. Stopped. And stared. "What happened to my room?"

Twisting her hands together, Maddy asked in a small voice, "You don't like it?"

The lace curtains were gone. The doilies were gone. The ruffled bedspread and canopy were gone. In their place was shimmering fabric decorated with wild swirls of blue and green. Air bubbles glistened in the weave, and hints of sinuous bodies and laughing dolphin mouths twisted in the patterns.

Framed posters from famous underwater movies adorned the walls and the grinning teddy bears on the bed—which Violet had always hated but couldn't bring herself to put in the closet—had been replaced by an enormous plush manatee and a smaller white harp seal pup.

"It's. . . ." Violet looked around, speechless.

"You hate it," Maddy offered, clearly trying not to be disappointed. "That's okay. We can shop together for something you like better."

"It's. . . ." She walked over and touched the plush manatee, remembering how the real ones had suckled on her fingers and bumped against her legs. Thinking of living in Florida forever. Never seeing Smitty again. Finally, she looked at Maddy. "It's perfect."

And to Violet's utter, horrified embarrassment, she burst into tears.

"So how was it, really?"

"It was fine," Smitty answered Brody's question with the same three words he'd used every other time he'd been asked about the trip. He waved his hand toward the waiting intern, and Ishmael slowly engaged the winch attached to the sea lion's crate. "I don't want to talk about it, okay?"

Thanks to the recent grants, Dolphin Friendly had a small mobile crane of its own for rescuing larger marine mammals stranded on land. Now they were pressing it into service for unloading Jasper. Fortunately, the crate slid out of the truck far more easily than it had gone in, and the sea lion was transferred to his temporary home without incident.

"Does he look funny to you?" Brody asked. "I know it's been a while since I've been this close to a California sea lion, but it seems like his belly is kind of . . . big."

Smitty shook his head, glad that Brody hadn't quizzed him harder about the trip. Though Jasper didn't seem permanently damaged by his frozen pizza orgy, he still looked a little on the funny side. Still, Smitty decided he'd rather talk about a gassy sea lion than Violet any day. "He looks the same as when we picked him up."

"Are you sure? He's not getting sick or anything is he?" Registering the tension in Brody's voice, Smitty glanced at his friend, noting the pinched skin around Brody's eyes and the nervous tapping of his index finger against his leg.

Brody was counting on the grand opening going well. He needed it to. Dolphin Friendly needed it to. Not only would it secure the second half of the funding, it would earn Brody's team the publicity they so desperately needed to be effective.

It was hard to educate the public when nobody had ever heard of you. Therefore, Dolphin Friendly needed some media attention. The gala would hopefully kick off their publicity drive with a bang, not a whimper.

Smitty reassured his friend. "He's fine. We'll give him an hour to settle in, then run him through the scissor behavior a few times to make sure it'll go smoothly when the time comes." Seeing that Brody was still unconvinced, he added, "Nothing will go wrong at the ceremony. I'll make sure of it myself."

"Hork, hork!" Having inspected his new surroundings, Jasper chimed in with a few healthy-sounding sea lion barks, and Smitty relaxed a fraction. "See? Even Jasper thinks it'll be a great show."

"Thanks Smitty. I owe you one." Brody clapped him on the shoulder. "I wasn't so sure it was a good idea to send you and Violet off on this job, but you guys pulled it off. I'm proud of you both." He paused. "Where is she, by the way? You didn't leave her in Florida, did you?"

As a joke, it hit a little too close to home, and Smitty winced. "No. She slept the last few hours while I drove. When we got here, she was so out of it that I asked Maddy to take her inside while we unloaded Jasper."

Now it was Brody's turn to wince. "I hope Violet's polite when she sees her room. Maddy spent days fixing it up and she'll be crushed if Violet hates it after all that hard work."

"Where is he? I'm going to kill him." Maddy's voice was muffled with distance, but the anger was unmistakable. There was an answering murmur, and in short order the two men saw a small, frizzy-haired dynamo stalking along the walkway that connected the inn to the Smugglers Cove Stranding Center.

"Looks like you're in trouble now, boss," Smitty observed, glad that someone else would soon join him in abject misery. "What did you do this time?"

"I have no idea," Brody muttered. He stepped towards his wife. "Honey? Is something wrong?"

She walked right past him and stopped in front of Smitty. "Wrong? Why would anything be wrong? Unless you count the fact that Violet's leaving."

Brody whispered, "Now who's in trouble?" before Maddy's words registered and he jerked back with shock. "Whaat?" He rounded on Smitty, standing shoulder to shoulder with his wife. "What happened? What did you say to her? Come on, Smitty, I sent you two down there to make up, not drive her away!"

"Me!" Smitty yelled. "How is this *my* fault? I tried to make up, I really did. We went to a water park. We talked about old times. We even went out to dinner . . . well, sort of. And we did this quiz in a magazine—except for the last question, which I made up—and we agreed that while we'd both been stupid, I'd been more stupid that she had." He took a breath and realized Brody and Maddy looked utterly confused. He let the breath out and said, "We made up. Really. It just wasn't enough."

"Why?" Brody asked. "Where is she going?"

"To work for Chaz the Amazing down at Seaquarium Florida. He's promised her a boat, a team, and all the manatees she can stand." Smitty kicked at a clamshell. "You know Violet and manatees. Who can compete with that?"

Though it had been a rhetorical question, Maddy answered, "You could, if you wanted to."

Smitty shrugged miserably. "I tried. I asked her not to go, but she really wants to."

"What exactly did you say to her when you asked her not to leave?" Maddy persisted.

"Um. I told her not to leave because . . ." Smitty searched his memory, remembered not being able to say the words he'd really meant, and finished with a mumbled, "Because Brody would miss her."

Maddy growled and Brody snorted. "Me? Why me? We went out maybe a half dozen times because it seemed to make logical sense that we'd work together. When she finally said we didn't have to bother anymore, I think I was more relieved than she was. Me and Violet were just never meant to be."

Smitty stared. "Then why the heck has she been such a bear ever since you and Maddy got married?"

Brody shrugged as if to say, *Who knows?* but Maddy answered, "Because everything was changing in the group, and she wasn't sure how to handle it. Brody found someone, and she was worried that you might be next."

"Me? Since when is she worried about *me* finding someone else?"

Maddy looked at Smitty as though she wanted to smack him for being so obtuse. "Since you married someone else while you were still in love with her, that's when."

"But that's ancient history," Smitty protested, not even bothering to protest the *love* thing, or wonder how Maddy knew.

"And they say that history has a way of repeating itself," Maddy replied. "But it isn't going to have a chance if she's down in Florida with this Chaz fellow, and you're up here."

Smitty rubbed a numb-feeling hand over his face and reminded himself to shave before the ceremony. He must look like a disaster.

A very confused disaster. Did he really have a chance? Or was this just Maddy being ultra-cheerful and believing in happily ever after, even for couples on the brink of disaster?

"Well, I guess that's enough of a lecture for right now. You do what you think is best," Maddy finally said. She surprised Smitty by stepping forward and kissing him on his furry cheek. "We're rooting for you, Scotty."

It felt like someone had kicked him in the chest. *Scotty.* "Nobody's called me that in years," he managed to say. Some days he barely even remembered he had a first name. He'd been Smitty forever.

Except that his mother had called him Scotty.

"I snuck it off your license one day out of curiosity. I hope you don't mind."

He shook his head, then found his voice, which cracked when he said, "No. I don't mind. I don't mind at all." He hugged his best friend's wife and said, "My family always called me Scotty. I guess that makes us family."

"Quit manhandling my wife," Brody ordered without heat, then hugged Smitty himself, with lots of manly back-slapping so the intimacy was okay. "Scotty."

"Not you too." Smitty groaned. "Let's just save that for special occasions, okay? Speaking of which. . . ." He glanced across the Smugglers Cove town commons towards a cluster of little shops, then over towards Jasper's tank as a plan took shape in his mind. "I may need your help with something."

Brody simply nodded. "Anything." He grinned. "What else is family for?"

Chapter Thirteen

Violet couldn't help herself. She sat next to Smitty at the opening ceremony. It was enough for her to be near him this one last time. It would have to be enough.

She'd blabbed about her job change to Maddy, amidst other tearful declarations she'd rather forget about, and had tendered her resignation officially to Brody not long after. He hadn't seemed surprised, so Violet assumed that either Smitty or Maddy had beaten her to it. Or both.

He hadn't asked her to reconsider, which had stung.

"Glad to know I'll be so sorely missed," she muttered, annoyed.

"What, Vi?" Smitty turned to her and she scowled harder. He looked amazing in a tux—always had. His studs and cuff links were a matched set of sterling fish she'd bought him three years ago for Christmas when they'd been getting along relatively well.

She stared at him for a moment, trying to memorize the way his blond-tipped hair waved across his forehead and the way the lines next to his eyes deepened when he smiled. Then she turned away. "Nothing important."

They fell silent as the lights in the new educational arena dimmed. The seats angled up on two sides from a central pool that would be used for rescued animals when the time came. A stage jutting out from one end of the glowing green pool would double as an exam table. A huge screen descended from the ceiling, and a spotlight hit Brody, who stood at the center of the stage.

Violet heard a lovesick sigh come from her other side and glanced at Maddy. She smiled. "Brody looks pretty good down there, doesn't he? Almost sexy."

Brody's wife shot back, "Not even *you* can ruin this moment for me, Violet." But she grinned as she said it, and Violet felt a pang that their friendship would be over just as it was beginning, because she was leaving as soon as the gala was over. She'd even called Chaz to confirm the job.

There'd been an oddly resigned note in his voice when he assured her that yes, indeed she was still welcome at Seaquaruim Florida. He even had part of her team assembled already.

Violet hoped she would like them.

Brody opened the ceremony by welcoming the various VIPs, particularly the members of the organizations and committees that had already donated to the Smugglers Cove Stranding Center. He then explained the center's mission by way of introducing the video that he and Maddy had put the finishing touches on just that morning.

The lights dimmed further and a glittering ocean appeared on the screen, which was visible from both sides of the arena.

"Brody flew in a film specialist from California to save it," Smitty whispered, and Violet didn't understand until she saw that video she'd shot the other day, the video that had set her and Smitty on their road trip.

Smitty's image smiled on the screen, the dolphins leaped and played at his command, and Violet felt her heart turn over in her chest. She saw the sun set behind him and turn his auburn hair to flames, and she felt tears threaten. It was that beautiful.

She felt Smitty take her hand. She didn't pull away when he laced their fingers together. She held on tight.

The screen dimmed for a moment and the audience murmured. Then Brody's voice rose in narration.

"Have you ever dreamed of the ocean? Of swimming through it fast as a jetski, or flying above it on seagulls' wings?"

On the screen, a montage of shots flowed past like water. Violet saw Smugglers Cove, saw *Streaker* forging her way through the Atlantic, saw herself tending a stranded seal pup with Smitty holding the frightened baby still for her.

Brody's amplified voice continued, "We have dreams like that, and so do the endangered marine mammals we represent." He went on to describe Dolphin Friendly and the goals of the stranding center. All the while, scenes flashed on the screen. There was a shot of the two of them on *Streaker*. Smitty's head tilted towards her and his teeth flashed as he laughed at a pair of playing humpbacks. Together, they pushed a stranded pilot whale out to sea. They stood shoulder to shoulder and waved as the whale headed for open ocean with a flick of its black flukes.

She heard a whisper from a few rows back. "That must be the married couple that runs Dolphin Friendly. Aren't they cute together?"

Maddy quivered, though whether from affront or amusement, Violet wasn't sure.

Married couple. Once, she had wished for it. Now it seemed impossible.

Brody continued. "Your generous funding makes possible programs like this. . . ." The screen showed Ishmael leading a group of school children through the animal care center and boosting a little girl up so she could see the baby seals more clearly. "And this. . . ." On the video, Ahab paddled in the water, surrounded by a pod of wild bottlenosed dolphins, a transcendent smile on his face. Brody's tone of voice shifted to one of amusement. "And of course, this." The scene shifted topside on *Streaker,* where Violet and Smitty could be seen hollering back and forth at each other until she walked over and attempted to push him overboard. Laughing, he fended off her hands until he could grab her by the waist and toss her in the water, following a moment later in a clean dive. They wrestled in the water while the bottlenoses chattered and splashed.

Violet sighed and felt those darn tears prickle again. What had felt like anger at the time looked an awful lot like love on the big screen. She wondered whether it was a trick of the camera.

"They *are* an awfully cute couple, don't you think?" Smitty whispered. He raised their joined hands to his lips.

The contact bloomed like a rose and she closed her eyes. Then she felt a tear leak from beneath her lids. "Darn it, Smitty."

"And now," boomed Brody's voice, "I'd like to introduce the members of Dolphin Friendly!"

The overhead lights came up as the video screen rose, and Smitty pulled her out of her chair. "That's us." They followed Ishmael, Ahab, and Maddy down to the stage, where the lights were so bright Violet had to squint. A stagehand pinned lapel microphones on each of them, in case they had to answer questions later on.

Brody introduced them and said a few words about their dedication, teamwork, and deep affection for each other. Violet snickered at that and Smitty poked her in the arm when the mike picked up the noise.

"And now, before we cut the ribbon that will signify the official opening of the Smugglers Cove Stranding Center," Brody proclaimed, "I would like to extend a special thanks to two of my best friends, two of the founding members of Dolphin Friendly, and two people I will sorely miss as I've recently learned they will be leaving Dolphin Friendly to pursue other interests. Violet? Smitty?" Brody waved them forward.

Smitty went. Violet didn't.

"What do you mean *two?*" Her voice rose to the

border of hysterical, but she didn't care. "Where's *he* going?"

Her question echoed throughout the arena, which was suddenly deathly quiet as the audience sensed impending drama.

Brody replied, "Smitty gave his notice today too. It seems he's taken a job with another team."

"He can't do that!" she cried, her voice squeaking. She stomped over and stood in front of Smitty. She put her face close to his and didn't care that the lapel microphones were amplifying every word. "You can't do that. Dolphin Friendly is your family. You can't leave the team."

He smiled gently and tapped a finger under her chin. "I could say the same for you too. You're as much a part of this as I am, but you're leaving. Aren't you?"

She thought of the brand-new condo in Florida. Then she thought about her room at the inn, all decorated just the way she would have done it herself, and she wavered.

Then she thought about the baby manatees in the tank at Seaquarium. About the scars on their backs and the very real threat of extinction.

Then she thought about Smitty finding someone else and leaving her alone.

"I'm going," she said firmly.

Smitty nodded. "Fine. Then so am I. Chaz is expecting us first thing Monday morning to inspect the new boat." He gently spun her around to face the audience, and tucked her against his side.

She didn't stay tucked for long. Just as Brody took a breath to continue his speech, she jumped back out of line and faced Smitty again. "You're coming to *Florida!*" Shivers of hot and cold raced through her at the thought. "You can't do that! How can I get over you if I still see you every day?"

She hadn't meant to blurt that out, particularly not over a loudspeaker in front of five hundred or so strangers. She winced at the echoes and the sudden flurry of whispers and giggles.

Smitty grinned. "I sincerely hope that you won't." He took her hands, holding them loosely. "You said earlier that Dolphin Friendly is my family, right? Well, they are. But even more so, *you're* my family, Violet. You always have been, even when I was too confused to know it. I love you."

This time, her lip trembled and a big, fat tear spilled over and slid down her cheek for all the world to see.

Violet didn't bother to brush it away.

Smitty looked startled and a little afraid. "Vi? Are you okay? You never cry."

She shook her head. "I've cried over you more

than once, you big dummy. I've just never let you see it before." She sighed. "I love you too, Smits. I always have, even when I was too mad to see it."

She went into his arms willingly, trembling a little, not quite ready to believe this was really happening. It could be a dream. She always dreamed about water. And Smitty.

This dream had both. With an addition.

"HORK! Buuuuurp."

A small tidal wave slopped over their feet as Jasper arrived on the scene. Smitty and Violet broke apart and stood side by side, trying not to laugh hysterically when the sea lion belched a second time. Brody would kill them if they lost it on-stage.

As it was, the audience was humming with Jasper's arrival, probably trying to decide if the animal was *supposed* to make noises like that.

"Here, I'll take that. Thanks, buddy." Smitty deftly retrieved a zippered baggie from Jasper's mouth and popped it open. He pulled a small, velvet-covered box free and Violet felt the bottom drop out of her world.

He dropped to one knee, clearly not caring in the slightest that his tuxedo pants were quickly soaked with salt water. He took her left hand.

"Violet, I asked you this once before when the timing was about as wrong as it could possibly be."

He paused as the microphone amplified his words and sent them to the farthest reaches of the arena. "I don't know that the timing's any better now, but I do know that I'm not spending another day without knowing you're mine." He glanced around and Violet saw Brody and Maddy give him thumbs up. "So I'm asking you in front of the rest of our family," he looked out at the audience, which was following his echoing words with rapt attention, "and five hundred people we've never met before. . . . Will you marry me? For good. Forever. Because you are everything to me. I love you."

Speechless, with tears streaming freely down her face, Violet nodded. He slid the ring onto her finger and she saw that it was a pair of white gold dolphins curled around a single diamond.

He stood and kissed her.

And this time it was no casual lipshake.

Epilogue

"Thar she blows!"

The hail should've been laughable, because there wasn't a crow's nest on the riverboat *Manny-T*, but Smitty just grinned and called, "What do you see, Ishmael?"

"*Trichechus manatus,* sir," came the prompt reply from the ex-intern, who was on loan to Dolphin Friendly South for a month.

"Manatees," cried Violet. She hustled up from below deck, where she'd been changing Eyebee.

The child had been christened James, but the members of Dolphin Friendly had quickly rechristened him Little Smitty, because the resemblance was so uncanny. That had evolved into Itty Bitty Smitty, which had been shortened to I.B. Violet and Smitty had given up the fight, and even called their son Eyebee at home. They figured the kid could blame his Godfather Brody for it when he got older.

Violet handed the six-month-old redhead to his father and leaned over the rail to get closer to her favorite creatures in all the waters of the world.

The animated brown pillows bumbled in her direction, waving their paddle-like flukes in greeting and snuffling at her with their soft, toothless mouths. Smitty grinned at the look of absolute rapture on his wife's face.

Ever since Brody had negotiated a merger with Chaz's group so they could exchange staff from Cape Cod and back again without paperwork, Smitty and Violet had commuted back and forth regularly, keeping up their research at Dolphin Friendly North while continuing to build the reputation and strength of Dolphin Friendly South.

It was a perfect arrangement.

"Gah!" Eyebee waved at his mother, and Violet reached for the baby as she slid over the side of the shallow-draft riverboat. Smitty tossed his son's floatee over the side and jumped in himself.

The manatees weren't disturbed by his cannonball entrance any more than they were by the baby tugging at their stiff whiskers. They were used to swimming with the Smith family.